LOVE
FROM
JOY

Also by Jenny Valentine

A Girl Called Joy

LOVE
FROM
JOY

JENNY VALENTINE

Illustrations by Claire Lefevre

SIMON & SCHUSTER

First published in Great Britain in 2021 by Simon & Schuster UK Ltd

1 3 5 7 9 10 8 6 4 2

Simon & Schuster UK Ltd
1st Floor, 222 Gray's Inn Road, London
WC1X 8HB

www.simonandschuster.co.uk
www.simonandschuster.com.au
www.simonandschuster.co.in

Simon & Schuster Australia, Sydney
Simon & Schuster India, New Delhi

A CIP catalogue record for this book is available from
the British Library.

PB ISBN 978-1-4711-9650-8
eBook ISBN 978-1-4711-9651-5
eAudio ISBN 978-1-3985-0009-9

This book is a work of fiction. Names, characters, places and
incidents are either the product of the author's imagination or are
used fictitiously. Any resemblance to actual people living or dead,
events or locales is entirely coincidental.

Typeset in the UK
Printed and bound by CPI Group (UK) Ltd, Croydon, CR0 4YY

*To friends in
kind places*

1

My name is Joy Applebloom, and I am ten years old. My family used to move around. A lot. We have slept by the sea and near rivers, on mountains and in forests. We have lived in the silent middle of nowhere and in non-stop noisy cities, sometimes where the sun doesn't shine for weeks, and sometimes where the sky is a never-ending, wall-to-wall blue. Together, we have been all over the world, but at the moment we live in one place and one place only, 48 Plane Tree Gardens, which is my grandad's house.

My big sister, Claude, says that 48 Plane Tree Gardens is the most boring place on Earth we could possibly have landed. According to her, we could not have picked a duller spot on the planet if we had tried. These days, Claude is very good at finding things dull and boring. It is one of her special skills. Luckily, seeing the good in them is one of mine. I have a nose for silver linings like a sniffer dog's. It might not be the Alhambra palace or a rollercoaster in the Nevada Desert or the glinting surface of the Indian Ocean, but I think 48 Plane Tree Gardens is still full of promise and surprises. The sun comes up in the front garden and goes down at the back, so it is always somewhere. We have our own front door and we are a five-minute walk away from all sorts of stuff worth doing. Grandad's house is warm and cosy and filled with cooking smells and piles of books and laundry drying and people I love. It's true that it is hard to find a quiet spot to do my homework, Claude reckons our clothes all stink of onions, the hot water is rarer than gold dust, and we probably are a tiny bit overcrowded, but we are all in one place together and so it is *home*.

Claude is three years older than me. She is tall and strong and she has shiny red hair and cold hands and very long eyelashes and a perfect nose. I am much shorter, and my arms and legs and eyelashes are quite spindly next to hers, like spiders' legs. Or twigs. But I have seen some incredible spiders, and twigs mostly grow into branches, so I'm quite confident that all I have to do is wait.

Even though I am on the small and cheerful side, I have some big and serious things on my mind. I am juggling them like a clown at the circus and I don't know yet if juggling is one of my special skills. I have made a list, so I can see how many things I'm supposed to keep in the air without dropping them.

NUMBER ONE: Claude has been grounded. This is the end of her actual world.

TWO: she is not talking to Mum and Dad. Not one single word. Grandad says this is called sending them to Coventry and I don't know why it's Coventry's fault but I do know that I would hate to get the silent treatment from my sister. It would be like getting locked out of a bright room.

NUMBER THREE: I think Grandad is lonely. Even his own cat has abandoned him.

NUMBER FOUR: my best friend, Benny,

is being bullied by a boy called Clark Watson. I don't know how long this has been going on, and I have no idea why, but lately Benny is being strangely jumpy and gloomy and quiet, and I am worried.

FIVE: I am on a mission to get my teacher, Mrs Hunter, to actually *like* me.

SIX: I am behind on my correspondence. I have a load of important letters I need to write and the pile is getting bigger every day.

Big thing **NUMBER SEVEN** is a top secret and very exciting plan about a birthday. I can't say one thing about it to a single soul or the secret will spring a leak and I will be a sieve and not a

clam. So, for now, I am having to send a certain person's birthday surprise to Coventry. Even if that certain person is so jumpy and gloomy and quiet that they don't seem interested in having a birthday coming up at all.

Oh, and **NUMBER EIGHT**: I have started *sleepwalking*.

It is extremely tricky trying to juggle eight things at once, especially when you are also having to be tidy, do your share of the washing-up and keep enough room in your head for school. But I have watched acrobats in Kazakhstan throw clay pots at each other at the same time as doing one-armed handstands, without one single breakage. I have seen travelling performers in Morocco balance goats on their shoulders and still keep thirteen skittles in the air. So I know that all of it is possible. I just have to do my best and try.

Claude has been dropping stuff all over the place since she got grounded. Yesterday she broke Grandad's *Home Sweet Home* cup, accidentally on purpose, and she's a total butterfingers for bad words. My furious big sister can swear in nine different languages and she is definitely making the most of that talent.

Being grounded means she can't leave the house, apart from for school, and she is not allowed to go on her phone or anything when she gets home again. This is because she has been sneaking around doing a whole lot of fun-sounding stuff she shouldn't, climbing in and out of our bedroom window when she is supposed to be asleep, and telling me that I have to keep my mouth shut so that Mum and Dad and Grandad don't find out.

Except now they have. Because of big thing number eight.

I was dreaming about being in a market. It was covered and hot and cramped and dusty and stacked all the way up to the ceiling with buckets and watermelons and blankets and crates of flowers and huge cuddly toys. It was just like the market we used to go to in Mumbai, where Claude couldn't stop sneezing because of the spices and her face was all scrunched up and quivery like a squirrel's and I laughed till I cried.

In the dream, I wasn't laughing and I wasn't crying either. I was opening and closing hundreds of teeny tiny drawers, searching for who-knows-what, and the drawers were getting teenier and tinier, and harder and harder to open, until my fingers were about as much use as balloons. The next thing I knew, I was awake and in the room

I share with Claude in real life. I was out of bed already and standing up in my pyjamas all the way over by the bookcase, and Mum and Dad were there too.

'Wow,' I said. 'Was I *sleepwalking*?'

I started telling them about the market dream because it was very vivid and still almost real in my head, but they weren't what I would call fascinated. Dad was leaning halfway out of the window and Mum was saying, 'Where the *hell* has she gone?' meaning my sister, and I had to admit I didn't know.

They looked scared, and that's not a thing I'm used to seeing, so I said, 'Sorry,' and then they said, 'What?' 'Did you know about this?' and I said, 'Well, yes. Sort of.'

Dad's frown swooped down on me like a vulture and Mum's lips went bone white. I got quietly back into bed and pulled the sheets up to my neck. There were no nets filled with drying chillies on the ceiling. No umbrellas or jangling cow bells or bicycle wheels. Not like in the market in Mumbai. Not like in my dream.

'And what exactly do you know?' they said together, at the same time.

'Nothing really,' I said, which was kind of true.

'It's MIDNIGHT,' Dad said, booming like a town clock.

'Has she done this before?' Mum asked, and I said, 'Maybe.'

'Oh, JOY,' Dad boomed again.

'Yes?'

'Why on earth didn't you tell us?'

'Because Claude told me not to.'

'That's not a good enough reason,' said Dad.

'It was a secret,' I said.

Mum shook her head. 'There are some secrets you keep, Joy,' she said, 'and some secrets you don't.'

This was news to me. It actually still is.

'*Really?*' I said. 'How do you tell the difference? How do you know which is which?'

They didn't answer my question, and Claude didn't answer her phone the fourteen times they rang it either

'Stay where you are,' they said to me, as if I had done the sleepwalking on purpose, or was thinking about following my sister out of the window. Then they left the room.

I concentrated on the wallpaper. Claude says the design choices at 48 Plane Tree Gardens are enough to keep anyone awake at night. But I have found that if I squint and get up extra-close, the flowers-that-look-like-cane-toads pattern in our bedroom is really quite relaxing. I must have just dropped off when Claude made her big entrance, head first and out of breath in the dark. She landed on the floor with a grunt, the exact moment that Mum and Dad burst in and switched the light on, which was a shock to all of us, and made my eyeballs want to hide in their sockets like crabs in their shells.

'Uh oh,' Claude said, getting up and trying quite hard to look serious. She wobbled a bit, and then she laughed, kind of to herself, like she'd just heard a joke. She smelled of cough sweets and bonfires and cola, and she blinked and squinted at us in the dazzling bright.

Mum took a long deep breath and spoke su-per-slow-ly, counting the spaces between every word. This is a thing that only happens when she is at the very outer limits of the known universe of being cross. It is rare, like a comet or an eclipse, and I think we are witnessing it more than we used to.

'*Where*,' she said, '*Have. You. Been?*'

Claude took her trainers off and chucked them on the floor. 'Out.'

'Out *where*?' Dad said, with his teeth pressed together, hardly opening his mouth, a ventriloquist on stage without a dummy. 'And with whom?'

'*Whom*?' Claude said, and she shrugged her shoulders. 'Just *out*.'

'Have you been DRINKING?' Mum said, and my sister snort-laughed, and said, 'NO,' and then everyone had another fight. This is something some people in my family have been practising a lot lately, and getting very good at, the same as me and fractions, because practice makes perfect, and I am really already so much better at those.

In between other, louder words, Mum said Claude was abusing her privileges, and Claude said, 'What privileges?'

Dad said Claude had broken their contract and abused their trust and that this was the last, the *very last straw, young lady*.

Claude made a shape like a teapot and said, 'Oh. You think?'

Mum said, 'You are *thirteen*,' and the teapot said, 'So?' It said all it wanted was its *freedom*.

Dad said, 'Freedom is something you *earn*.'

Claude stuck her fingers in her ears and shouted, 'Oh, yeah? Really? WHY?' and then Mum threw her hands in the air and stormed out of the room and Dad just stood there like he'd missed the last train and wasn't at all sure what was supposed to happen next.

My sister followed Mum into the corridor to

have the last word. She likes having those. I had my pillow over my ears by then, like a hat, but it was still pretty loud.

She yelled, 'I HATE YOU,' and Mum yelled, 'FINE.'

Then Dad said the thing about Claude being grounded and she squealed like she'd just been stung by a wasp.

I think that's what woke Grandad up.

He came out of his bedroom with his hair fluffed up like a spring cloud and his pyjamas buttoned all the way up to the neck. I could see him through the doorway from where I was sitting in bed. I haven't known Thomas Ernest Blake that long, but sometimes I love him so much my heart feels like popcorn cooking in my chest. I waved at him, the only other not-furious person in the building, but he couldn't see me without his glasses, so he didn't wave back.

'What's going on?' he said.

Mum and Dad and Claude all shouted, 'NOTHING!' like they were on the same side suddenly, and Grandad should be minding his own business, in his own house, in the middle of the night.

'Oh, good,' he said. 'So can you all stop doing it, then?'

He shuffled back inside his room. Mum and Dad stomped down the stairs to where they sleep on the sofa and Claude threw herself onto our mattress so hard that my whole body lifted off for a second, like a magic trick, like I was just lying on a bed of mid-air.

'Again!' I said, and she growled.

'Don't speak to me.'

'What? Why not?'

'This is all your fault,' she said.

'Is it?' I said. 'How?'

Claude put the pillow over her head and squealed into it some more, and when she finally spoke, her voice came out all muffled and squashed and flat. 'Why couldn't you just do as you were told?'

'*Me*?'

'Yes. *You*. How hard is it to stay in bed like you're supposed to?'

'I was *asleep*,' I told her. 'I didn't know about the sleepwalking because I wasn't *awake*.' Claude's face was so close to mine I could see the hairs between her eyebrows and the tiny saffron flecks in the whites of her eyes.

She said, 'I'm never talking to them again. Ever.'

'*To whom*?' I said, because I thought it would

18

make her laugh, but it didn't.

'*Them*,' she said. 'Mum and Dad. You're lucky I'm still talking to you.'

'Me? It was an *accident*. I didn't sleepwalk on *purpose*.'

'Well, now I'm *stuck* here,' she said. 'In this *prison*. So thanks a lot.'

She put the pillow like a wall between us so I couldn't see her any more. Not a glimpse.

'It's not a prison,' I told her.

And on the other side of the border she said, 'It is to me.'

2

The sun shone brightly through our curtains the next morning, but my sister was still a raging storm. I was hoping that she would feel better after a good night's sleep, and I knew for certain that she'd had one of those, because of the snoring. My beautiful big sister snored all night like a warthog who keeps remembering a hilarious joke.

'Morning,' I said, but she didn't reply.

I rolled over to face her. 'I had a dream that an armadillo was teaching you geography.'

Nothing.

'What is your geography teacher called? Do they look anything like an armadillo?'

Again. Nothing. Claude frowned and kept her eyes closed, and told me to stop talking, using only her face.

'Claude?' I said. 'Are you still grumpy?'

One eye opened. One eye, as sharp and beady as a laser, but no mouth.

There is more than one way of helping Claude out of a bad mood. Sugar sometimes helps. An arm-tickle is quite reliable. I have a whole menu of impressions that usually do the trick. But this morning, absolutely nothing was working. My last butter mint was rejected, she snatched her arm away when I went to touch it, and not one of my impressions made a difference, not even the one of Dad when he has got something in his eye and hops about on one leg for no reason, which is her go-to favourite. Claude groaned and put her whole pillow over her face, and kicked her feet really fast under the covers like she was swimming.

'I can't *believe* I'm GROUNDED,' she said.

'Maybe you're not,' I told her. 'Maybe they changed their minds.'

'No way,' she said.

'You never know.'

Claude came out from under the pillow and blinked at me. Her eyes were bright balls of fury. 'You know what they are?'

'What?'

'Fascist dictators,' she said.

'Really?'

'I hate them,' she said.

'No, you don't!'

'Well, I'm not talking to them. And I'm not getting up and I'm not going to school either.'

She rolled over to face the wall and her breathing went all slow like she had gone back to sleep.

'Claude,' I said.

'Nope,' she mumbled. 'I'm on strike.'

'That's just going to get you in more trouble.'

One shoulder shrugged. 'So?' she said. 'How much worse can it get? They've already robbed me of my freedom.'

'Come on,' I said, pulling at her arm. It was all floppy like a ragdoll. 'Let's go and have breakfast.'

'No chance,' she said. 'I'm staying here for the rest of my life.'

I had to use my emergency strategy to get her to change her mind. This involves talking wall-to-wall non-stop nonsense until she has to leave the room for some peace. I don't have to do it very often. It really is only for extreme cases. And it works every time.

I said, 'How easy do you think it would be to replace somebody with a robot? How many different sections are there in our spines? I think Dad is getting a bad back from sleeping on the sofa. If he was a robot, would he get a bad back? Or would he *fake* one to be convincing? Do you think Grandad ever gets a bad back? He stands up super-straight all the time, like a pencil. Have you noticed that? Mrs Hunter would give him a gold star for posture. She stands like a sack of potatoes but I wouldn't say that to her face because I am trying to get her to like me. Do your teachers like you? Who is your favourite? Have you even got one? Do you think Mum was ever in trouble at school? Do you think pickled walnuts are disgusting or delicious or weirdly in between? If you had a dog, what would you call it? Is it true that everyone has got one eye bigger than the other?' And so on.

I talked without hardly breathing until Claude rolled over onto her back. She opened one eye and used it to look at the ceiling.

'Enough,' she said. 'You win. I'm up,' and she threw back the covers and thundered out of the room.

When I got downstairs, she was pulverizing innocent cornflakes with the back of her spoon, Mum was doing something on our laptop and Dad was hanging up crumpled sheets. The atmosphere in the kitchen was about as warm and welcoming as a floor-to-ceiling block of ice. At least Grandad was smiling, with his hair all combed and his shoes so shiny the cat could see his face in them. Grandad's cat is called Buster. He is extremely handsome, and he loves nothing more than gazing at his own reflection. It is his absolute all-time first-choice thing to do.

'Hello,' I said to all of them, Buster included.

Grandad said, 'Good morning, Joy,' and after that it was so quiet I think I could hear the bubbles popping on the surface of Mum's tea.

I packed my school bag and put it by the door. I brushed my hair, sort of, and had a look in the fridge.

'Are you three friends again yet?' I said to the rest of my family.

Claude glared at me. 'Tell them,' she said, 'that it is actually against my basic human rights to keep me inside against my will.'

'We can hear you,' Dad said.

'Tell them,' Claude said again, 'that I am not actually talking to them.'

Mum snapped the laptop shut like a trap. She said, 'Well, you're still grounded.'

'Tell them,' Claude said, looking at me, 'that this is an infringement of my civil liberties. Tell them that I will not live under a tyrannical regime.'

'Maybe you should just tell us you're sorry,' Dad said, and he sail-cracked another sheet.

Claude didn't tell me to tell them anything after that.

I poured myself the last little dribble of orange juice and Grandad cut a slice of bread for me and put it in the toaster. While I waited for it to pop up, I pretended I wasn't having plain old toast and a measly teaspoon of juice for breakfast. I was having pancakes with syrup, or a two-egg omelette, or porridge with a runny-honey smiley face. I was having tamarind rice cakes with coconut sauce or samosas with chilli chutney, or a fresh mango, fizzing with flavour and just pulled from a tree.

'Is it done yet?' I asked, and something stuck very low down in the bottom of the toaster started burning, and nobody said a word.

3

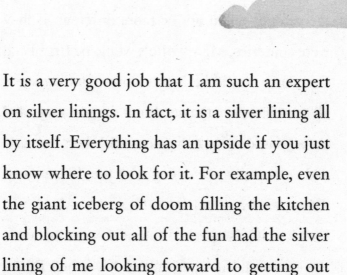

It is a very good job that I am such an expert on silver linings. In fact, it is a silver lining all by itself. Everything has an upside if you just know where to look for it. For example, even the giant iceberg of doom filling the kitchen and blocking out all of the fun had the silver lining of me looking forward to getting out of the house. Iceberg, bad. Walking to school, good. It's simple.

Buster came with me as far as Miss Wolfe's garden, and then he leaped up and high-beamed along her front wall with his tail flipping backwards and forwards like a sea snake.

Miss Wolfe lives on the other side of the street at number 57. Her house has the same grey front door and small square windows as number 48, but the gardens could not be more different. If they were countries, Miss Wolfe's would be Brazil and Grandad's would be North Korea. His garden is all straight and organized and mainly grey, and not a lot is allowed to happen, while hers is messy and colourful and teeming with life, like a party. There are bees and butterflies everywhere you look and it is so packed full of flowers that even the air around it smells nicer. I watched Buster lick his lips and flex his teeth, and his eyes glinted like the blade of a knife.

'Be good,' I said into his swivelling ears. 'Be kind to other creatures and please look after Grandad while we are out.'

I am not one hundred per cent positive that he heard me.

Mum or Dad used to keep me company on my walk to school, but now I know the way, I mostly do it by myself. On the short bit of the main road that I walk down, there are shops and cafés and two hairdressers and a gym. Outside the train station, which breathes people in and out like a tide, there is a stall that sells fruit piled up in bright pyramids and rainbow towers. After the fruit stall, I go past a park with black railings and baby swings and a seesaw and a funny sort of rocking horse on a big spring that isn't shaped like a horse at all, but a giant parrot. There are real-life parrots in the trees too, little grass-green parakeets with berry-red beaks. In India, those birds are all over the place, although I don't think I have ever seen an actual park. Not really. Here, they flit about in the branches, a tiny glimpse of our old life come to visit our new. When I am walking past, I imagine all the other things there would be, as well as the little parakeets, if this was a park in India. I layer things over what I am

really looking at, like transfers, until I get it right. Cows, wandering down the middle of the road with bells and necklaces on. Strings of marigolds and magnolia on the railings, and little black taxis that look like the only kind of car you can draw when you are six. Red dust, and women in bright saris, and four people on a motorbike, at least, and a tangle of wires overhead, like spaghetti with squid ink. Trucks all brightly painted, sounding their horns on repeat, and bicycles with man-sized stacks of flattened carboard on the saddles, and the smell of chai and hot sugar and exhaust fumes and incense. A skinny dog driven mad with fleas, and rubbish like you wouldn't believe, and everything moving, and more wires, and music, and a thousand extra people for every step.

My walk goes by in a flash, like time travel. After I have finished walking in India, I am right around the corner from school.

You can tell when you're nearly there because of the oak tree that towers over the rooftops like a giant. It waves at me every morning from the far end of the street. It is a thousand years old so it has been there for a long time, way before anything else, the street included, and the school and the railings and the houses, and probably even the park. I am very keen on that oak tree. It has done me a lot of favours. It introduced me to my new best friend, Benny Hooper, for a start.

It made me and my teacher Mrs Hunter agree on something for the first time ever. It helped me become a member of the Historical Society and I really do love belonging to things. Me and Benny and Mrs Hunter and Grandad are all members, which is proof that even very different people can have a lot in common. When Benny and I found out that the council wanted to chop the tree down, we started a campaign to save it. It's not over yet, because campaigns can take ages, but I think we might be winning.

School was hard at the beginning, because I had never even set foot in one before, and I couldn't put one foot right. It isn't always easy. I forget the rules sometimes, because there are so

many. And trying to get Mrs Hunter to tolerate me is still a bit of a challenge. This has a lot to do with me talking too much and not being the most brilliant at sitting still, and also getting in a lot of trouble for climbing the thousand-year-old tree and hiding out in it when I wasn't supposed to. But that was a long time ago. I am much better at all the rules than I used to be, and I am crossing my fingers that any day now Mrs Hunter will really start to notice.

I like it here, I really do. For lots of reasons. Like how good I am getting at maths and back bends. And how there are so many people, from so many different places, that it can sometimes feel like being all over the world again, in all of my favourite places, at the same time. My new friends' families come from Ghana and Nairobi and Iran and Somalia and Milan and Kosovo and

38

Karachi and Syria and Paris. And that's just the ones in my year. Sometimes when the corridors are full of people and everyone is talking, it's like being at a soukh in Marrakech or on the Metro in Paris or at the seaside in Barcelona or on a busy street in Lima, Peru, all at once. There are forty different languages in this one school. Even the United Nations only speaks six. When I tell Benny this, he says exactly what I am thinking, which is, 'WOW. This place is like the PLANET in miniature. It's like the whole world on the head of a *pin*.'

Apart from Benny, that is my absolute favourite thing about it.

4

Benny Hooper read somewhere that parakeets like the smell of apples, and that if you hold out some chopped apple in your palm and stand very still, they will fly down and perch on you in the hope of a snack. We wanted to try it. So we walked a big loop from his house to Grandad's house, with the park in between.

As soon as we got to the gates, Benny picked up a big stick and started swinging it about and passing it from one hand to the other. Once or twice he looked like he might be going to throw it for an invisible dog, but he didn't let go, not even while we were trying to tempt the birds out of the trees, not even when we gave up and ate half the chopped-up apple ourselves and left the other half on the grass for them to enjoy in peace later. Then, nearly at Plane Tree Gardens, outside the shop where you can buy everything from shoe polish to cat food, there was a bollard leaning over a big yawning hole in the ground. It looked like it might topple, any second, almost as if it had been waiting, and Benny wedged the stick down into the hole to straighten it, and left it there holding up the bollard, and kept on walking. He didn't miss a beat, not one step. He didn't even look back.

I did, though. I stopped and I laughed out loud and he said, 'What? What's funny?'

'That!'

'What?'

I pointed at the bollard. 'That was amazing,' I said.

Benny grinned at me. 'What do you mean?'

'I couldn't work out why you had that stick with you the whole way. It was a mystery.'

'Oh.'

'And then there it was,' I told him. 'The reason for the stick. That bollard. Waiting for you. But right at the end. Like you knew it was coming. Did you know it was coming?'

Benny pulled a face and shook his head. '*No*.'

'WOW,' I said, and Benny laughed.

'You're funny,' he said.

'And you're a bit magic,' I told him, because I

really think he is.

Benny changed school for me, overnight. Thanks to him, I went from being fish-out-of-water-ish and lonely to being someone who belonged. And it's not just school that he changed for the better. It is everything. I honestly think he might be the best best friend I have ever had. This is why I want to make sure that he is all right, and why I am very seriously starting to worry that he isn't.

Benny notices the exact same things in the world as I do, like the delicate skeleton of a leaf, or the thousands of ways dogs are like their owners, or how a stepped-in puddle at night can look like a photo of the Milky Way. From the moment I met him in the playground, from the very first thing he said to me, about a tiny acorn having just what it needs to turn into an enormous oak, Benny and

I have seen eye to eye, and treasure *everywhere*.

At the moment we are almost non-stop searching for treasure. It is one of our top five favourite things to do. This is because of a thing we saw on the internet about a boy who discovered a valuable Roman coin in his very own back garden. We dig around the edges of the playground or at the bottom of Benny's building or, best of all, in Grandad's garden at number 48. Benny wants to be an archaeologist. He really does believe that there is treasure everywhere, like I believe in silver linings. According to him, priceless stuff is just a few metres away underneath us, wherever we are, at all times.

I tell him that Claude says the exact same thing, but about rats.

So far, we have dug up a brown glass medicine bottle, a 1p coin from 1976, a rusty old key, some bits of broken plate, a toy soldier with one arm missing, two chipped marbles, a dinner fork and an empty travel tin of lemon sherbets. We haven't found anything Roman or priceless but we are not giving up yet. Not me and Benny Hooper. Not even close.

Sometimes I think a thing right before Benny says it, like, 'That cloud looks like an upside-down umbrella,' or, 'In all seriousness, don't you think that magnets are actually *incredible*?'

Sometimes we talk at the same time, at a thousand miles a minute, and sometimes we are so busy and quiet we realize we haven't said anything at all. We are both vegetarians and we both love chocolate and we both know nearly all the flags of the world and what countries they belong to. And Benny has a definite talent for spotting silver linings. He is almost as good at it as me.

Benny says that I have changed stuff for him too, in lots of ways, and that all of them are good.

He likes having a friend who has been to so many places and seen so many things.

He says, 'I have never met anyone who knows as much about killer whales or train timetables or what snakes like to eat as you do.'

He says, 'Nobody else I know has been inside a volcano or under a waterfall or on top of a camel, and you've done all three.'

He says that I make people interested in things because I am so interested in them. He says that kind of thing is catching. According to Benny, I am the bug that everybody wants to get.

I like it when he says that. Some people wouldn't want to be compared to a contagious disease, but I take it as a compliment, the best compliment, because I know that's how it is meant.

Benny says I make break time fun, because I always have a plan. He says I even make lessons less boring because I talk about stuff.

'Mrs Hunter wants me to *stop* talking,' I tell him, and Benny smiles and pushes his glasses up his nose and says, 'Well, *I* don't.'

Benny sticks his tongue out, just a tiny bit, when he is working hard on a maths question. He frowns when he is reading and when he is talking on the phone, and when he isn't happy his eyes get ten shades darker in the time it takes to blink, like there is an eclipse of the sun happening inside his own head. His hands are square and they are mind-bogglingly spine-tinglingly brilliant at playing the piano. Benny's house is full of musical instruments. Everyone in his family can play. He writes his own comic books about a boy called Nut and they are exciting and funny and terrifying in all the right places. He is always making things and he is a very good cook. Sometimes, at his house, when he is getting us a snack, he lifts the big wooden spice box out of the bottom cupboard and uses a bit of everything, and it is like watching a wizard making a spell.

Benny hums when he is eating, and he likes the shady edges of the playground as much as I do, and I have noticed that he always tries to be the last one to leave the classroom so he can switch off the lights. He has been going to our school since he was *five*. His big brother Sam went there too, four years before him. Even Benny's mum and dad went there, but Benny's mum says that was a 'very, ve-ry' long time ago. Benny asks her if Mrs Hunter was their teacher, and she laughs and taps him on the nose with her pointing finger and says, 'Nope.' She also says that Mrs Hunter is one of the best teachers on the staff, and one of the nicest people you could ever meet. Benny looks at me then with his face all stretched and his glasses balancing on the very end of his nose, like she has just told us there are cream cakes the size of hippos living on the moon. But his mum doesn't smile and she is not joking and I can tell by her eyes (which are just like Benny's) that she thinks it is completely and totally true.

5

Benny's mum is called Angela. She is an artist and her paintings are big and loud and quick and strange, and she has lots of different jobs and one of them is to work sometimes in the school canteen. She has a laugh that makes you want to start laughing and a walk that looks like a dance. Her wrists are loud with bangles and she wears bright flowy clothes that remind me of rainforest birds and sweet wrappers.

Wherever Angela is, it feels like somebody just turned up the colour.

Benny and Sam and Angela and Ed, who is Benny's dad, live in the flat that Angela was born and grew up in, on the Meadows Estate. The label on their doorbell says,

THE HOOPERS

Their block is called Sunningdale. This is the perfect name for it because on a good day all the rooms are full of sunshine. It is high up on the eleventh floor and the view is breathtaking and enormous. I have spent hours looking out of Benny's windows. You can see the parakeet park, and the high street stretching all the way down to the roundabout with the giant mangled goalpost sculpture in the middle. You can see the quick glint of the faraway river in between things, and the neat rows of houses in Plane Tree Gardens and cars inching around on the roads, and the fancy pink-and-white birthday cake mansion near the doctor's surgery.

When the fair came to the park, we could see all the rides and the stalls and the big wheel, lit up and flashing, and the people with their noisy mouths like dots and their arms flailing. One minute we were right down in it, breaking toffee apples inside their wrappers and screaming our heads off on the Wurlitzer and breathing in hot-dog steam and jumping out of our skins on the ghost train. The next, we were watching it all from above, like gliders or eagles or gods. We could see where we had only just been walking, in the narrow path between the bumper cars and the place where you have to go fishing with tiny magnets to win a giant panda. The Wurlitzer was no bigger than my thumb.

I spend a lot of time at Benny's house. Angela says I am already part of the furniture. She says I can come here whenever I like, so at the moment, I do. 114 Sunningdale is full of laughter and music and stories and loud family card games and even louder family conversations, and jokes and the smell of cooking and the bustle of eating, and dancing in the kitchen and stretching out on the massive sofa to read a book or watch cartoons. There are shoes everywhere, not always in pairs, and roller skates for doorstops, and sometimes Ed comes into the room talking through a megaphone, just because. Sam is really cheerful for an older brother. He plays the cello and takes his headphones off when I am talking to him and he laughs at most of my jokes. He calls Benny *Grandmaster B* and he is always putting his arm around him, always kind to him, just because. Sam lets Benny borrow stuff without threatening to kill him if he drops, scratches or breaks it. He loves the Nut comics and he can sit through a whole family conversation without yawning, crying or storming out of the room. Being with the Hoopers is just like being at our house when we are talking to each other, and not calling people fascist dictators and not having to eat breakfast on an iceberg. All rowdy and free and lumped in together and having a great time.

Angela knows that we have done nothing but move around the world since I was born. She says it must have been incredible, and that she is a bit jealous, and can only imagine. I have been learning that this also works the other way round. Staying in the same place has given Benny's family very strong roots. Angela and Ed and Benny and Sam know *everyone*. They can't go five metres without someone saying hello. Benny's parents' best friends are people they went to school with, people they have known since they were three or four. Angela and Ed were friends when they were ten, which is thirty years ago at least, and the exact same age as me and Benny are now. Angela says Benny's dad was a very good roller skater and wore short blue shorts and long white socks that still make her laugh when she thinks about them.

She says, 'I will dig you out a photo. You won't believe your own eyes.'

'Imagine meeting your husband when you are *ten*,' I tell Claude, and she laughs and does this little song about how I'm going to marry Benny, and I don't say a word because honestly, I will not mind if I do.

When we came back to be with Grandad, Claude said we would turn into sticks in the mud. She said she would miss the beaches in Zanzibar and the mountains in Peru and the forests in Costa Rica and California and France. She said we would miss the vans and huts and boats and tents and rooms we slept in, the markets and temples and museums where we lost and found each other again. She said we would be stuck and muddy and freezing and bored.

She said, 'This place is going to be a great big land mass of nothing. Guaranteed.'

But I watch Benny's family finish each other's sentences and drop everything to look at the sunset and turn their sitting room into an actual orchestra and cut up the last piece of cake into five little pieces so we can all have a bite, and tell jokes at the dinner table until they are laughing so much they can't get the food in their own mouths, and I know that if you put your whole heart into it, same as anything, being sticks in the mud is an excellent thing to be.

6

Being best friends with Benny is nearly wall-to-wall silver linings. But I'm afraid that Clark Watson is Benny's tornado on the horizon, with a guarantee of rain. Clark and Benny used to be friends and now they are not. That is all I know because it is all Benny will tell me. I don't know what Benny has done to annoy Clark Watson. I don't know if even Benny knows. But it is definitely something. Because he is most definitely annoyed.

Clark Watson goes to the same school as us. We are in the same class. He also lives in Benny's building, on the ground floor, at number 9. So him not being Benny's friend any more is *everywhere*. He is wiry and small and his hands are pale and non-stop busy, like quick fish in a tank. In lessons he can be loud enough that sometimes Mrs Hunter can't hear herself think, but in the playground, he speaks so quietly you have to lean in very close and listen if you want to hear him. The meaner the words he uses, the quieter he gets. It is the sort of thing that the villain in Benny's comic books would do.

These days, whenever Clark is nearby, Benny gets smaller and is just generally less *Benny*. It's as if he is watching himself from the outside and doesn't like what he sees. He shrinks, and the little frown line on his face that is shaped like a comma disappears and goes all smooth like it was never even there. I have only seen this happen twice before: once when a baby elephant on TV headed the wrong way all alone to get lost in a sandstorm, and once when we went on the ghost train at the fair. Twice is enough to know that the comma on Benny's forehead vanishes when he is sad or afraid.

Clark Watson has a big brother called Jet. He is the same age as Claude so I ask her if she knows him, from school. We are putting the knives and forks away after dinner, and I drop it into the conversation, just when I am dropping the tin opener into the drawer.

Claude pulls a face. '*Jet Watson?*' she says. 'How do you know *him*?'

'I don't. Benny knows his little brother. Sort of.'

She shakes her head. 'Jet Watson is *weird*.'

When I ask her what sort of weird, she says, 'He is the kind of person Mum and Dad lie awake at night worrying I am friends with, when my friends are nothing like him at all.'

'What do they worry about exactly?'

Claude breathes out extra-patiently and tucks her hair behind her ear on one side. She is wearing gold hoop earrings that are so big I think I could fit my whole arm through them.

'I can't explain all this to you,' she says. 'When you're my age, you'll just *know*.'

'Have you ever spoken to him?'

'Who?'

'Jet Watson.'

'Of course not.'

'Why not?'

'I don't hang around with him. I told you.'

'Well, does anybody?'

Claude rolls her eyes. 'I have no clue.'

Sometimes I wish Claude could be the teeniest tiniest bit more observant.

'Why are you asking me anyway?' she says, and I tell her about Clark and Benny and how they used to be friends and now they're just not.

I say, 'I'm trying to find out, you know.'

'Find out what?'

'The *reason*. Like maybe Clark is being mean to Benny because he is bored or unhappy,' I say. 'Or both. Or maybe it's because Mrs Hunter clearly thinks Benny is amazing and Clark Watson isn't. I know how *that one* feels.'

'Maybe he's just horrible,' Claude says. 'Maybe he enjoys it.'

'Really?' I say. 'You think?'

'Yep. Really.'

Claude pushes the cutlery drawer shut with her bum. She has finished listening. But I haven't finished thinking. Maybe Clark Watson wishes that he was as good as Benny at the piano or as clever at maths or as super-helpful in the classroom or as fast a runner. Maybe he doesn't like it that Benny's new best friend is a girl, i.e. me. Maybe he is jealous. There could be hundreds of reasons for the way Clark is acting, and he is keeping them all extremely well hidden and locked away in the deep dark underground, like a chest full of Roman coins.

I think about all the stuff I don't know about Clark and why he's being horrible to Benny. And for some reason, that gets me wondering what it would be like if all the hidden things in the world got found out suddenly, in one single moment. I think about all the secrets I know. Good ones and bad ones. And then I think about all the ones I *don't* know, and what on earth they might be. It's like swimming in the ocean and knowing that there are miles and miles of water underneath you, all the way down to where it is midnight-dark and no one has ever even *been*. I wonder who might be keeping these secret secrets, the ones I don't even know exist, and I think it would be an enormous thing, to dive down and see them all out in the open at once, like long lost shipwrecks. I wonder if it would be a wet weekend or a festival of silver linings, a burden or a relief, or even both.

7

Now that I have settled in a bit to my new school and routine, I've started letter writing again. I used to do it a lot, but I haven't really had time since we moved. That's about to change. I might have found my best ever friend, and lots of new ones, but that doesn't mean I will let myself forget anyone else, in all the other places I have been. I am still keen to hear what everyone has been doing and to share all of my news, and so I am determined to try to keep up, in different time zones, every day of the week.

Eiji, my best friend in Tokyo, has his own phone and sends me funny messages on my dad's phone in the middle of the night (which is when Eiji is on his way to school because for him it is morning). And some people, like Joseph and Prosper in Zanzibar and Anita in Delhi, have email, but others, like Ruby in Ho Chi Minh, or Björg in Iceland prefer a letter. When you've travelled around the world as much as we have, letters are a good way to stay in touch with all your old friends. You can take your time over them, and draw pictures. You can start writing them before breakfast and go back to them after lunch and finish them off at bedtime. Lucy and Olivia write to me from Arequipa. Johanna writes from

Norway. Thille sends postcards from Amsterdam. And I have made a resolution to *always* write back. I am getting good at the twenty-four-hour clock and I don't mind sending messages or emails. Sometimes it is impossible to get a turn on the computer because Mum and Dad are so busy with work and Claude says she needs it for chatting to her friends (disguised as writing an essay about the human reproductive system). But that's fine, because it turns out that my favourite way of staying in touch is writing real letters. I love when they arrive too, addressed to me on the doormat at 48 Plane Tree Gardens, in all sorts of different envelopes, with beautiful bright stamps.

Claude calls me old fashioned, and says that I am from the *Dark Ages*, but some of my friends don't even have the internet, or their own phones, so it's the only way to reach them. My sister has just as many friends scattered around as I do, probably more. Our friends are *everywhere*. When we grow up they are going to be in so many places that we will be able to travel the whole world all over again and never feel alone. One day in the future, Joseph and Prosper and I will have a glass of fresh lemonade on their concrete veranda. Fabiola will take me back to play hide-and-seek in the garden at Frida Kahlo's blue house in Mexico City. Ruben and Nasreen and I will make bright Rangolis with coloured sand on the just-swept floor of their big yard in Chhattisgarh. In Vietnam, Nelly's mum will make me a hot batch of melt-in-the mouth vegetable dumplings. Brad will laugh until he is nearly sick at all of my jokes on the Staten Island Ferry. And Sophie will ride with me down the side of a big snow-capped French mountain on our rickety bikes with the wind whipping our hair and filling our ears until they sing.

Proper letter-writing is a slow business, and I am flat-out busy and already behind, but it is worth it.

8

I can't help wondering about what Grandad does all day long when the rest of us are out. I have been trying to imagine how it must feel to spend that much time by yourself, with nobody to talk to apart from a self-obsessed and painfully good-looking cat who is only there part-time and whose listening skills are about a hundred times worse than mine.

I don't think Grandad worries much about

Grandad. This might be because he has been mainly worrying about Buster. He thinks the cat is off his food.

I say, 'He looks one hundred per cent fine to me,' and he does, all glossy and fluffed up and pleased with himself. He is licking his lips and soaking up all the attention he is getting. Buster adores being talked about. You can tell.

Grandad says that Buster hasn't touched his food in nearly two days.

He says, 'It is very unlike him.'

He is going to call the vet because he thinks Buster might be sick, but I don't. I have never seen a sick cat look so healthy and flawless and alive. It is a mystery.

When I ask Claude what she thinks Grandad does with his time, she says that he mostly gathers dust. I find this funny because she is the one who lies on the sofa without moving for so long that sometimes I have to check she's still breathing. When I talk to Mum and Dad about it they say that Grandad is *fine*, but in a way that means they have too much on their plates already to be worrying about that as well. It is clear that juggling big thing number three is going to be completely up to me. If Grandad is stuck at the top of lonely mountain, I am going to have to come up with my own way to help him down.

First, I need to find out if he has any undiscovered interests. I am going to have to dig for them like treasure, because they might be just what I need to solve the problem. But the digging doesn't really go to plan. At dinner, Claude is very busy carrying on using me as a go-between to communicate with the fascist dictatorship. Sometimes I wish that she would be a bit more like Benny's Sam, and maybe hug me just because she feels like it, or smile at Mum, or pay even a tiny bit of attention to what Grandad is saying. But at the moment, wishing isn't going to make it happen. It is too much of a mountain for my sister to climb.

'Joy,' she says. 'Please ask Dad to pass me the ketchup.'

'Joy, please tell Mum to stop touching my foot under the table. It is giving me the creeps.'

In between all the go-between-ing and message-passing, I just about manage to ask Grandad what his top five favourite hobbies are. He looks at his plate for so long before he answers that I think he might have forgotten the question. I am crossing my fingers for ballroom dancing or tightrope walking or lion taming. This is another pointless wish.

'Joy,' Claude says. 'Please tell Mum or Dad that I can't eat this macaroni cheese because I have just this minute decided to be a gluten-free vegan.'

'How convenient,' says Mum, and Dad says, 'Oh, well, that's just great.'

'Reading,' Grandad tells me, looking at me over the top of his glasses, and I say, 'Great. What else?'

'Joy,' Claude says. 'Please remind our parents that principles are more important than convenience.'

'That's rich,' Dad says, and Mum makes a comment about fast fashion, and how many times a certain person wants to go shopping.

Claude is grinding her jaw. I can hear it.

'Birdwatching?' Grandad says. 'Oh! The Historical Society, of course.'

'Joy,' Claude says, pushing her uneaten food

across the table and leaning back in her chair until the two front legs come up off the ground and she's balancing there. 'Please tell the Lords and Masters that I have finished and if it is *convenient*, I am getting the hell out of here and going upstairs to do absolutely nothing that's worth doing because I don't even have access to my own phone.'

'That's three so far,' I say, ignoring her because I am trying very hard to focus on Grandad. 'Have you got any more?'

'Take your plate to the sink,' Mum says to Claude, and Claude says, 'Joy, please inform our mother that I would like her to use the word please when addressing me, as demonstrated above.'

Mum says she doesn't think Claude is in a position to teach anyone about manners.

'*Seriously?*' Claude says, landing her chair with

a bang, before she remembers she isn't talking directly to Mum. 'Joy, please tell my accuser that she should think twice before making such false allegations.'

'Do you know,' Grandad says, 'I think I might quite like to take up gardening.'

'Interesting,' I say, which is when Claude falls out with me as well, for not doing my job properly.

'How useless are you?' she says, and I am about to answer when Dad says, 'That's a rhetorical question, Joy.

'What does *rhetorical* mean?'

'It means you don't need to dignify it with a response.'

I am always happy to learn a new word.

'Sorry, Claude,' I say. 'I was just trying to have a nice talk with Grandad. But if it helps at all, I'm sure Mum and Dad heard you.'

'Yes,' Mum says. 'Unfortunately, we did.'

Claude leaves the room with a bang and stomps up the stairs. Mum and Dad clear the table and slam some cupboard doors in the kitchen and I'm fairly certain that the knives and forks get dropped from quite a distance into the sink. 48 Plane Tree Gardens is an angry orchestra. Everyone is making so much noise that I can hardly even hear Grandad say his fifth hobby, which is called Solitaire and is a game for one person, and no use for solving a loneliness problem at all.

9

Meanwhile, Benny is shrinking and getting quieter. Things in that department are only getting worse. The other day, Clark Watson had fun throwing stuff at us when we were on our way up the stairs at Sunningdale. First he threw food and then he threw some dirt and then he threw stones and one actually stung like a bite when it hit me. Thankfully, he is not a very good shot, so it was just the one. After he threw everything, he hid. Badly. Benny pretended it wasn't actually happening, even when we were ducking to avoid cold chips and a fistful of grit. I am about as good at pretending as Clark Watson is at hiding. I hopped about like the floor was hot lava and made noises that even I wasn't expecting, and even though I couldn't see him, I shouted,

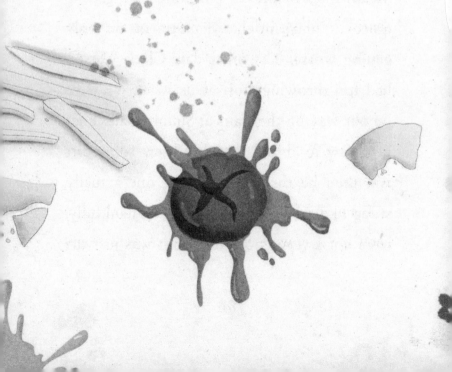

'Clark Watson! What are you throwing stuff at us for?!' And all that time, Benny kept his head down and moved smoothly and quietly up the stairs, like he was somewhere else entirely, most probably an escalator, and nowhere near to Clark Watson or me.

'Why did you do that?' I asked him when we got to his yellow front door. I could hear music coming through the letterbox. I could see bright shapes moving on the other side of the rippled sunrise of glass. Inside 114 Sunningdale, it was another great day on Planet Earth. But out here, on the doorstep, it was a very wet weekend.

'Do what?' Benny said.

'*That!* Why did you ignore Clark and just let it happen?'

Benny held his hands out, palms up, as if to show me they were empty. His eyes were empty too, like all the lights had gone out. Benny was having a power cut, but he didn't have any candles. It was a terrible sight to see.

'I don't know what else to do,' he said.

'How long has he been picking on you?' I asked, and Benny shrugged. 'Not long. A while.'

'Why???' I say, and Benny shrugged again and said nothing.

'Have you told your mum and dad?' I asked him.

'No,' Benny said. 'I don't want to.'

'Why not?' I said.

'It's not that bad,' he said

'Okay. Sam, then,' I said. 'Does he know?'

Benny shrugged.

'He must have noticed something,' I said, and Benny scratched his head.

'He did ask,' he said.

'And?'

'I told him I have a bad stomach.'

'Why?' I said. 'If Sam was my big brother, I wouldn't keep Clark Watson a secret.'

'Would you tell Claude?' Benny said.

'Probably. Definitely. She'd make mincemeat of someone who was bullying me.'

Benny shuddered. 'That's what I'm worried about.'

'What?

'If I tell Sam, or my mum and dad, or Mrs Hunter, even, Clark will be in big trouble.'

'Yes.'

'And then he'll hate me even more.' Benny shook his head. 'It's not that bad,' he said for the second time, and I don't think either of us believed it. 'Telling tales will just make it worse.'

I didn't point out that doing nothing wasn't

exactly making it better. I kept it zipped because I could see that Benny just needed to go inside and make a snack and watch some cartoons and forget about it.

But forgetting about it isn't working. At school this week, Benny has 'forgotten' his lunch money and 'lost' his school bag, and 'dropped' his new phone, which is actually Sam's old one, but still, new to Benny, who is not a forgetful or clumsy person, and who also likes lunch, very, *very* much.

Mrs Hunter says, 'What are we going to do with you, Benny Hooper?' and he looks at his shoes, all scuffed and muddy on the stinky school carpet, and says, like it is his fault, 'I honestly do not know.'

I am not sure that Benny *is* being honest about how bad it is. I am completely one hundred per cent certain that you-know-who took his lunch money, and threw his bag over a wall, and broke his new phone. This is the saddest and most afraid I have ever seen him. It is like the Benny I know is being buried under something heavy and he is trying his best to clamber out but he is just too tired.

So I start digging.

Because he hasn't got any lunch, we share my cheese-and-cucumber sandwich, my bag of cherry tomatoes and a banana muffin. While we are sharing, I ask him some questions about Clark Watson, like, 'Have you always known him?' and, 'Is his brother friends with your brother?' and, 'Does he have any other friends?'

Benny just shrugs. And chews. He is being about as enthusiastic as Claude.

I say, 'Does your mum know you broke your

phone?' and Benny shrugs again.

I say, 'Where did you last see your school bag?'

I say, 'Where is your lunch money exactly?'

Benny has less than nothing to say. He seems very interested in the writing on the side of my juice box, for much longer than it should actually be taking to read.

This is not the Benny I am used to having lunch with. He has shrugged more in this one conversation than in the whole entire time I have known him. He is hiding from me and he does not want to be found, just like Clark Watson's kind side, and Mrs Hunter's approval, and Claude's sense of humour, and Grandad's cat, and Mum and Dad's actually *listening*, and all the other things that are missing or hidden or sneaking about in the deep and murky dark.

Benny is too afraid of Clark to tell the truth

about what is happening, and I think he wants me to agree with him and join in. I am supposed to block my ears and cover my eyes and seal my lips and keep my nose out, because Benny doesn't want anyone to know or talk or even think about the problem. This must be an example of a secret you are absolutely not allowed to tell, even when you want to, even when you think you should. I am not sure I'm going to be any good at those. I am not at all sure I am the kind of person who can watch her best *best* friend shrinking before her eyes and do nothing to fix it.

But instead of saying what I really think, I change the subject.

I talk about how fast greyhounds and whippets can run. I ask Benny what kind of dog he would get if he was allowed one. And what animal he would be if he could pick one. I ask him why

Labradoodles aren't called Poobradors. I give him an update on the Buster situation. I do all of this because when you are looking for real buried treasure, you have to dig very carefully. You have to go slowly and use special spoons and little pencils and tiny brushes that move aside specks of dust, one at a time. You can't just race ahead and wave a big shovel around and uncover the prize. That's not how it works.

Rare and precious things are no good to anyone if they are smashed to smithereens.

10

After school we go to Benny's house. Our journey up the stairs this time is uneventful. Nobody throws anything and nobody gets stung by stone wasps and I for one am extremely relieved. Inside, Benny's dad Ed is listening to a piece of music with my name in it. He is conducting an invisible orchestra in the sitting room and the volume is turned up mind-bendingly loud. I am trying to work out if it might be a good idea or the right time to try and talk to him about Benny, and how worried and sad he is, but Ed has his eyes closed inside the music, and he wouldn't be able to hear me even if I shouted about Clark Watson at the top of my voice.

Angela comes in with a bowl of green apples that are the exact same colour as the scarf she is wearing in her hair.

'AH,' she yells, over some trumpets. '"ODE TO JOY". HOW BRILLIANT. DO YOU LIKE IT?'

I make the shape of the word 'YES' with my mouth and I nod at the same time.

She hands me an apple. She has gold rings on her fingers and gold hoops in her ears.

She looks around the room. She makes the

shape of 'WHERE'S BENNY?' and I point to the bathroom.

'OH,' she says, and she taps Ed on the arm so he opens his eyes and stops conducting and turns the orchestra down a smidge. It is still loud, but now at least I can hear myself think. Benny's mum and dad nod at each other and then they both move a bit closer to me.

'We need to ask you something,' Angela says.

'Okay.'

For a second, I think this is going to be about the Clark problem, but then I realize it can't be, because they are smiling. They are as filled with happiness and light as two sunbeams. I am almost disappointed.

'We,' says Ed, 'have had an *idea*.'

'For Benny's birthday,' says Angela. 'We want your opinion.'

Benny's birthday is in less than two weeks and he is going to be eleven. This is a very big deal and something to get very excited about, in my opinion. But anyone would think Benny Hooper was allergic to getting excited about birthday celebrations. That is how little he seems to want to talk or think about it.

Thankfully, his mum and dad have other ideas. They are still beaming at me.

'We've been wondering about a surprise party,' Angela says.

'Wow,' I say. 'Really?'

'Yes,' she says, and Ed says, 'What do you think?' and then Benny's mum says, 'Sam is all for it. He said to talk to you because we need a *theme* and you will know what it is.'

I start making a picture of it in my head. There are banners and flags and silly party hats and an enormous cake. There are people singing and dancing and playing games. There are drinks in paper cups and an actual punch bowl and a piñata and a chocolate fountain and maybe even a band. I think maybe it is happening at 114 Sunningdale, or maybe outside, in the street.

And that's when something brilliant pops into my head. It sparkles like diamonds. It glints like gold coins.

'OOOOH,' I tell them. 'I think I do have an idea.'

Ed and Angela's smiles get even wider. 'Tell us!' they say together. They are whispering and shouting at the same time, and the music is still loud and there is no sign of Benny yet. Ed does a little drum roll on a bookshelf in anticipation.

'How about a treasure hunt?' I say.

'That's *it*!' Benny's mum and dad clap their

hands together with delight and Angela does a little turn on the spot like she is dancing.

Ed says, 'We *knew* you'd be the best person to help us,' and Angela says, 'Oh, that is *brilliant*. You are so creative and clever!'

And then quickly, because I think we can hear Benny coming back from the loo, she says, 'We were thinking about getting him a metal detector. What do you think?'

'*Seriously?*'

'Seriously.'

Now it is my turn to dance on the spot. Benny's eyes will *pop* when he sees it. He will feel like the luckiest boy on Earth. I cannot think of one thing more guaranteed to cheer him up.

'PERFECT,' I say, and then Benny is back and we are all eating apples and conducting the violins and pretending to be the person on the big bass drum, like nothing has happened. Benny lurks a bit in the doorway. I know he is trying to hide a red mark on his forehead that is suspiciously the size of Clark Watson's thumb.

'Benny?' Angela says, extra-loud and extra-cheerful to cover up our secret chat. 'Come over here. What are you up to?'

He shuffles across the floor with his hat half-pulled down over his eyes. His bottom lip is sticking out like a shelf.

Ed laughs and tickles him under his chin. 'I don't know what's got into you this week, son.'

I want to tell him that the answer is on the ground floor of Sunningdale but Benny gives me a quick dark look that means, *Don't you dare.* So I don't. But I do give him a look back that says, *I won't keep my mouth shut for ever.*

11

As if I didn't already have enough letters to write, I have realized that there are even more that I need to finish and deliver, much closer to home. Firstly, I have written one to my teacher, Mrs Hunter, which is burning a hole in my school bag, and may or may not be the kind of letter that you write but never send. And right now I am considering writing her another one just about the Benny problem, although I haven't made up my mind about that yet. It's hard to go behind someone's back and against their wishes, even if you are doing it to help them. It's not a black-and-white decision to make.

Then, on top of that, there are all the invitations to Benny's surprise birthday treasure hunt. And I am halfway through a note to Miss Wolfe at 57 Plane Tree Gardens, about a certain four-legged someone called Buster and a certain two-legged someone called Thomas Ernest Blake.

Grandad might be worrying about Buster's health, but I'm not. I don't think his cat is sick at all, I just think he isn't *hungry*, because he is busy getting double rations. That is my theory anyway.

I think Buster has started disappearing to Miss Wolfe's house for sleepovers. I am guessing that he has graduated from outside in her beautiful garden to inside her sitting room, on her comfortable sofa. He has been going missing for longer and longer stretches of time, and when he saunters back in without an explanation, he definitely does not look like he's been having fights or sleeping under a hedge. He looks sleek and satisfied and well-rested. He smells of perfume and drops the odd bit of cushion fluff. Grandad doesn't wear perfume or enjoy a fluffy cushion, so I think that is evidence – exhibits A and B.

I have started observing Miss Wolfe, so I can get some more information, and see if my theory about Buster is right. She lives on her own, and she doesn't leave the street very much. She is small and quite round and she has short grey hair and very dark twinkly eyes that make me think of hedgehogs. Sometimes she goes to the shop on the corner, but that's about it. I have observed her coming back from there with bags of cat food and this is why I am pretty sure that Buster is her new part-time lodger, because Miss Wolfe doesn't have a cat. I am also pretty sure that Buster is no fool, because the cat food Miss Wolfe buys is the fancy kind that comes in little foil trays with pictures of blow-dried kittens on the top, and he is not getting that kind of treatment around here.

The problem with my theory being right is that it is doing less than nothing to help Grandad with his loneliness problem, and that's why I am writing to Miss Wolfe. I have chosen some paper that is covered down one side with bugs and flowers, and I am using a grass-green pen that smells of apples because I think she will like it. I want to tell her what I know and still stay on her good side. I am trying to keep it short and snappy, but friendly too, so she is not discouraged.

Dear Miss Wolfe,

It is very nice that Buster comes to visit you so often. I am sure he is very grateful for the fancy food, and it's all fine, really, but I want you to know that he already has an owner — your neighbour, my grandad, Mr Thomas Ernest Blake, from number 48. Maybe you could invite him over too? He has lots of time on his hands, he would like to learn all about gardening, and he is very fond of a Bakewell tart.

Love from Joy x

I put it through her door in the morning, on my way to school, and make a little wish that it does what it's supposed to. I peek through the letterbox to make sure it has landed safely on the mat. The inside of her house smells of clean sheets and honeysuckle and traces of a certain familiar perfume. From where I am crouching, I can see the corner of a fluffy cushion on the sofa and a shiny silver cat bowl on the kitchen floor. The bowl has its own mat underneath, bright red like famous people's carpets. No wonder Buster is feeling so at home over there.

I have very high hopes for my letter. In our Save the Tree campaign at the Historical Society, Grandad talked a lot about the power of the written word. So here goes. My fingers are crossed that the power of mine will bring him and Miss Wolfe together, and solve two loneliness problems in one single go. I am excited to see what Miss Wolfe will wear at their wedding. I can already picture Buster carrying the rings in a jingly little pouch attached to his collar.

12

Claude might not be talking to Mum and Dad, but she is non-stop talking to me, and this week it is mainly about different bits of her body. This is not what I would call riveting, but it is highly strange. Apparently, according to her, she is so monstrous, it is a miracle she can even show herself in public without people screaming in terror and running for their lives. She makes me stand in front of the mirror with her and talks me through all the things that aren't right. She also talks a lot about a boy called Riddle, who I have met once, a while ago, when me and Benny went to the fair. He is called Riddle because his name is Jamal Riddler. I think this is the perfect name for him because why Claude likes him is one hundred per cent a mystery to me. He mumbles a lot and wears a hairband. I'm pretty sure he is Claude's boyfriend. She acts very strangely and not at all like herself around him. The real Claude would tell Riddle to speak up, and tell funnier jokes, and try harder at just about everything if he wants to even *think* about impressing her. But the Claude that I saw when he was there looked uncomfortable in her own skin, like she had forgotten how to do simple things like walk or smile or hold a paper cup or eat candyfloss or use a seat belt.

I stand in front of the mirror with my sister

and I remind her that she is smart and funny and clever and has lots of other talents that are way better and more important than being nice to look at. I tell her that she is not at all a hideous monster. I say all the right things, but she stares at me like I am not making any sense. She is trying on jeans. She has to stand on the bed to get a proper view.

'Riddle thinks I look better in skirts,' she says out of nowhere.

I tell her I bet Riddle looks better in skirts too.

'You like jeans,' I say. 'You *love* them.'

'Yes, but Riddle doesn't.'

'Well, who cares what *he* thinks?' I ask.

'I do.'

'Why?' I ask her.

'Why what?'

'What's so golden about Riddle's opinion?'

Claude frowns. 'Good question.' She is really

thinking about it.

'So? What's the answer?' I say.

She puts her sweatpants back on and jumps down off the bed. 'I'll have to get back to you,' she says, 'because I don't even know.'

After that, while we are lying on the floor and Claude is drawing faces and I am colouring them in, she starts talking about Mum and Dad. She doesn't look at me while she is speaking. She says our parents are *having problems* and she says that's why they are acting so weird all the time and she says that they are going to get a *divorce*. This word turns my stomach into a glass of bubble tea and makes me want her to stop talking and being nice to me and just be quiet and go back to looking like she's died on the sofa.

'They aren't even married, are they?' I say. 'They can't get divorced.'

'Well.' Claude holds her not-drawing hand out, palm up, like she is showing me something. 'You know what I mean.'

'How do you know they are having problems?' I say, and she says, 'Oh, come on. It doesn't take a genius.'

She says, 'They are never in the same room for more than five minutes and they are always furious and busy.'

'Really?'

'Really.'

'I thought that was work stuff.'

'Yes. Well, it's making them miserable. And now they don't love each other any more. And they're taking it out on me.'

'No, they aren't.'

'I'm *grounded*,' she says.

'You're not grounded because Mum and

Dad don't love each other,' I tell her. 'You're grounded because you climbed in the window after midnight and got caught.'

'Whatever,' Claude says, which is the closest she is ever going to get to admitting that I'm right.

13

On Saturday morning, Claude is upstairs sulking about being grounded and Mum and Dad are out somewhere possibly not loving each other any more. I am waiting for Benny to come over so we can go and look for priceless antiques in the flower beds at the park. Grandad is alone in the kitchen, leafing through some Historical Society pamphlets. One is about the grand opening of the library in 1879. One is about the train station. And one is about parks and trees, and that's got our school oak tree on the cover. I am standing outside by the front door. It is quiet on the street, with no traffic and not even a breeze. All I can hear is Grandad, at the other end of the house, loudly sighing.

I close the front door to go and find out why the leaflets are making him so unhappy. Maybe they are full of misprints and spelling mistakes. I know from experience that Thomas Editor Blake is not at all fine about those. Punctuation and grammar should probably be on his list of favourite hobbies. But when I walk into the kitchen, it is not Historical Society print-outs he is holding, it is Buster. He strokes his beloved, unfaithful cat. Buster is just about putting up with it, like being constantly adored takes real patience.

Grandad looks into his eyes and says, 'What's got into you, little fellow?' and I say, 'I think you should have a word with Miss Wolfe about that.'

I don't tell him about my letter. I keep that under my hat. There are some secrets you should tell and some you shouldn't.

'Who?' Grandad says, blinking up at me.

'Miss Wolfe.'

He looks at me blankly.

'She lives at number 57. Across the road,' I tell him. 'With the nice garden.'

'Well, what about her?'

I say, 'Do you know her?'

'Not really.'

'Well, Buster does,' I tell him, as delicately as possible. 'I think they might be friends.'

Buster jumps off his lap and lands gracefully and soundlessly on the floor. Grandad smiles. His smile says, *Buster is friends with lots of people. He is a dynamic, popular cat.*

'I think she might be feeding him,' I say.

'Oh.' Grandad stops smiling. 'Do you?'

I've started now, so I finish. 'Yes. And I think maybe he stays over.'

'Really?'

'Two or three nights a week.'

Grandad is staring at Buster, who doesn't look even the tiniest bit sick. Or guilty. Or interested. He cleans his whiskers with his elegant paws and sniffs snootily at his plate of untouched, low-price food. He blinks. And yawns. We are boring him. His tongue is sea-urchin pink.

'Sorry,' I say. 'But I think Miss Wolfe is slowly kidnapping your cat.'

Grandad pulls a face. His eyebrows lift and separate like Tower Bridge. We are quiet for half a minute. Buster stretches each of his legs, one at a time, front first, then back. He is in no kind of hurry. He points his toes captivatingly, like a dancer.

'Feeding him, eh?' Grandad says.

'Yes. The posh stuff. In foil packets. With fluffy cats on the lids.'

'Right.' He tickles Buster behind his perfect, ungrateful ears. 'I see.'

I tickle Buster too. He is incredibly soft and impossibly beautiful. His purr rumbles like there is a tube train running through his middle. I can't help picturing the passengers as mice.

'At least this means he's not sick,' I say.

'Yes,' Grandad says, not smiling but not

frowning either. 'I hadn't thought of that.'

He picks up Buster's breakfast and gives it a light sniff. 'I wouldn't eat that either,' he says, and he lets it slide off the plate into the bin.

'We could buy some fancier food,' I tell him. 'That might do the trick.'

'Yes. Or I could shut him in.'

'Like Claude?'

'Yes,' Grandad says, then he looks sternly into Buster's eyes and says, 'You're GROUNDED.'

'You wouldn't,' I say, and he shakes his head.

'No. I wouldn't.'

Buster starts purring and rolls over onto his back, quick and curly like one of those fortune-telling fish you put on your palm. He could not care less about this problem if he tried. His fortune fish would read: *Not even a tiny bit bothered at all.*

'Perhaps I should go and have a word with this Miss Wolfe,' Grandad says.

'What kind of word?' I ask.

He looks like he is thinking.

'Would you do it nicely?' I say. 'She does seem very twinkly and kind.'

'Of *course*,' he says. 'I am a very nice person. I am extremely well-mannered and polite.'

'Oh, yes,' I say. 'Of course. You very much are.'

I'm not feeling good about getting an old lady into trouble, and I do actually want them to be friends, so I say, 'If it helps, I don't think it's strictly Miss Wolfe's fault.'

'No?'

'I think Buster keeps her company,' I tell him. 'I think she is lonely.'

'*Lonely?*' he says, like he has never even

heard of the word, and then it is my turn to Tower Bridge my eyebrows, and I say, '*Yes.*'

'So Buster is being kind,' he says, which is not the first word I would use to describe him.

'Yes,' I say. 'Exactly.'

'In that case I think I'll sleep on it,' Grandad says.

'What does that do?'

'It gives me time.'

'For what?'

'To find out the full story.'

'The full story?'

'People do things,' Grandad says, 'and it's not always obvious why.'

'Okay. Is it the same with cats too?'

'I am going to think it through, and make sure I don't jump to the wrong conclusions about this Miss Wolfe and my beloved Buster.'

'That sounds very wise,' I say, and I am not just thinking about Miss Wolfe or Grandad or the cat any more, I am thinking more than ever about Benny and Clark.

14

Even with the *divorce* word hanging over us, it is lovely spending proper time with my sister. I really do quite like it when she is banned from having a phone. We make origami animals and talk about all kinds of stuff like we used to: planets and football and marine biology and Ancient Egypt. Sailing and the constellations and books she thinks I should read.

I tell her that I am secretly trying to fix Grandad

up with a girlfriend, which she says is *gross* and I say is *helpful*. I tell her a bit more about the Benny problem. Claude has a way of looking at things that is extra to mine, the same way two torches are better than one in the dark. She is never scared of people like Clark Watson. She is fearless and good at standing up to big things. One of the first things I remember about being alive is Claude swimming like a crocodile in a paddling pool in Colombia, snapping at the bright blue water with her sharp white teeth at a gang of boys who were trying to splash me. She is also astonishingly good at origami. She makes three owls and a rabbit in the time it takes me to make one wonky zebra.

'I'm going to have to make friends with him,' I tell her.

'Who?'

'I told you. Clark. Jet Watson's little brother.'

Claude blows her hair out of her eyes. She rubs her face with the palms of her hands. She says, 'What are you on about?'

'It's the only way I can think of to stop him picking on Benny.'

She is staring very intently at the instructions for making a flying eagle.

'Continue,' she says. 'Explain.'

'Well, if Clark Watson was still his friend, then Benny wouldn't have lost his school bag or his phone or his lunch money. And he wouldn't be so quiet and secretive and worried and sad and un-Benny-ish.'

Claude yawns and stretches. 'That sounds like Benny's problem.'

'*It is* Benny's problem. And I am Benny's best friend. So I'm going to have to fix it.'

'You?'

'Yes. Me.'

Claude turns to face me. 'How are you going to manage that?' she says.

'I already said. I'm going to make friends with him.'

'Are you serious?'

'Well, he must have some good points.'

Claude says, 'That's what *you* think.'

And she is right. I do. Even though the signs right now might be pointing to zero, I am trying to be on the lookout for reasons that Clark Watson isn't all bad. I am trying to stay sure that *nobody* is, because that's what I have always believed, and I don't want to have to stop. Take Grandad, for example. He is pretty much all good sides, even though at the beginning, when we came to stay, I couldn't find them because he was too busy telling me to tidy up and not to touch about a million different things, and to stay out of the way on the stairs, *for pity's sake*. Or Mrs Hunter, who is mostly angry when you first meet her, but is actually quite shy, and doesn't sleep very well, and has sore knees, and a soft spot for caterpillars, and could do with a holiday. Maybe Clark likes running or chocolate cake or going fishing in the canal. Maybe he is into origami or flying kites or hamsters.

I say, 'I won't know until I ask.'

'Let me get this straight,' says Claude. 'You're going to say, *Hello, Clark, let's be friends, love from Joy*?'

'Something like that.'

And it is almost true. In my head, I have been trying to write Clark Watson a letter.

I am not sure how to start it, so I'll just go with: *Hello, Clark.*

Maybe I will write: *It's Joy here. I know we don't speak much, and I hope I'm not being a total nosy parker, but are you okay?*

Or maybe I will try: *I am quite keen to find out what your hobbies and talents are. Do you like swimming? Are you interested in books? What are your thoughts on fancy dress? Are you secretly a really talented actor? Card player? Long-distance runner?*

What I really want to ask is: *Why did you fall out with Benny? Do you throw things at him because you are bored? Do you want to help us look for treasure? We would happily split our findings with you three ways.*

When I tell Claude this, she laughs and rolls over on the bedroom carpet onto her back.

'You deserve a medal,' she says.

'For what?'

'For always having your glass half-full.'

'What does *that* mean?'

Claude tells me, while her perfect paper eagle circles overhead, that some people see a glass that's half-empty, and some people see it half-full.

'It's the same glass,' she says, 'but people look at it differently.'

'That,' I say, 'is pretty amazing.'

'I'm the first kind,' Claude says. 'I'm the empty kind.'

'Do you think so?'

'I *know* so,' Claude says, sitting up and coiling all her shiny red hair on top of her head like a giant conker. 'And do you know what you are, Joy?'

'What am I?'

'The *third* kind.'

'*Is* there a third kind?

'Yep. And it's the best one.'

'Well, what is it?'

'It's when you're grateful for the glass.'

I guess it is true that I see only good when sometimes other people see problems.

Like on a bright morning when Grandad tuts about the mucky streaks that show up on the windows, but I just see the sun. Or when Mum's laptop runs out of battery so she can't finish the vital and mind-numbing thing she's been doing, but I'm glad because it means she'll spend more time with me. Or when Claude gets annoyed that there are so many green sweets in the packet because she hates green ones with a passion, and they happen to be my favourite. Or the time we had a power cut and Dad was ranting about the government and I just loved the way the candles made every room look golden and flickery and exciting, like the whole of Grandad's house had turned into a birthday cake.

'Thanks, Claude,' I say. 'That's the nicest thing anyone has said since Benny called me contagious.'

And my sister laughs and says, 'See?' because apparently even that is proving her point.

So now I am thinking about this letter to Clark Watson too, as well as all the others, from breakfast to supper, and during every other conversation I am having, and while I am cleaning my teeth and looking for my pyjamas and getting into bed. It is a non-stop, all-day rumble, like Buster's purring. In my head the letter I write to him is perfect, and fixes everything. But that's my head. And even I know that sometimes life is not as easy and as grateful for the glass as that.

15

At school, in the hall, 5J do a class assembly. They act out lots of scenes, and Tumelo, who is the tallest boy in Year Five, plays the part of a policeman. Mrs Jackson, who is 5J's teacher, plays an old lady in a big grey wig and keeps forgetting her lines. At the end, the whole class opens out a big banner which says,

SPEAK UP,
BE KIND AND
TELL THE TRUTH!
HELP SOMEBODY
TODAY!

I can still see it even when my are eyes closed, like when you hold something up against the too-bright sun. The banner is burned into my eyeballs, so I can't ignore it, and it is telling me exactly what to do.

136

To start with, at morning break, I stay behind and ask to speak to Mrs Hunter. Benny gives me a quizzing look and the rest of the class file out into the corridor, and Mrs Hunter sighs and looks at her watch and says, 'What can I do for you, Joy?'

I give her the letter that has been hiding for ages at the bottom of my bag. It is a bit damp and crumpled and it looks as if something might have been nibbling the corners of the envelope.

'I wrote this a while ago,' I say. 'And I've been carrying it around with me. Sorry.'

Mrs Hunter holds the envelope between her pointing finger and her thumb, like it is something she has just pulled out of the drain. 'What is it?' she says.

'It's a letter.'

'I can see that it's a letter,' she says. 'But why are you giving me a letter when you see me almost every day?'

'It's a thank-you letter,' I say. 'I wanted to thank you.'

Mrs Hunter looks quite bewildered.

'*Thank* me?' she says. 'What for?'

I look at the letter that she is still holding like the back leg of a frog. I'm not sure why she is asking me all these questions when she could just open it and find out.

'For being my teacher,' I tell her. 'For being kind to caterpillars and knowing so much about nature-y things. For joining the Historical Society and working hard to save our school tree. And for helping me understand the point of fractions. And queuing.'

'Oh,' she says. 'That's my job, Joy. That's okay.'

'And for getting used to me?' I say, sort of like a question. 'And giving me the benefit of the doubt?'

Mrs Hunter blinks.

'I know you are tired and your knees hurt,' I tell her. 'And I know I'm a big chatterbox and you mostly just want a bit of peace and quiet.'

Mrs Hunter's eyebrows can't get any higher. If they did, they would be hovering like matching millipedes above her head.

'But I really do like school now,' I say. 'And I like you too. I just wanted you to know that.'

Mrs Hunter is a bit lost for words. She looks in her handbag for something she doesn't find, and she drops the letter in without reading it and then she says, 'What a nice thing to say, Joy.'

'I don't think there is a single spelling mistake in there,' I tell her. 'And I think it's probably about an eight out of ten for punctuation.'

'Well, it's ten out of ten for effort,' she says.

She even smiles, which makes me very nearly open my mouth and spill the beans about Benny. But at the very last minute I change my mind. I want to speak to Benny before I do it, and not just give away his private secrets behind his back. I don't want my best friend to feel I have let him down when all I am really trying to do is help. So I tell Mrs Hunter I am going to make my own T-shirt with the words BE KIND written on the front. I say, 'I think it should be our new school uniform,' and her smile flickers out like a candle. I'm not sure she can take any more from me at this moment. She is looking like she could do with sitting down.

Out in the playground, Benny asks me where I have been.

'Speaking truth to Mrs Hunter,' I tell him. 'In a good way.'

He looks worried. As usual. There is a bruise on his forearm, he has bags under his eyes, and his clothes look like they have been dragged through a puddle.

'Get ready,' I tell him.

'Why?' he says. 'What for?'

'You're next.'

'What do you mean?' he says, and I say, 'Benny. You are extremely brilliant and popular and funny and caring and clever. You have lots of friends and loads to smile about. Your family are amazing. You even have a very important birthday coming up. But right now, you are nothing but miserable and unhappy.'

Benny's bottom lip wobbles.

I say, 'I know you don't want to tell anyone

else what is happening.'

He pushes his glasses back up his nose.

'But I am your *best friend* and I am here to help you.'

Benny sniffs. A single tear slides under his glasses and down his cheek, all on its own.

I squeeze his hand and I don't give up. 'We have to try and fix the Clark Watson problem together.'

He looks at me and then at his new favourite place to look, which is the floor, and says in a small voice, 'Yes. We do.'

'And if we can't,' I tell him, 'we are going to have to speak up and tell the truth and ask somebody for help.'

16

Instead of going to Sunningdale after school, I go straight home to keep Grandad company. While I walk, I try to concentrate on something upbeat and positive, which is Benny's secret surprise treasure hunt birthday plan. I am determined to make it extra-special so it will cheer him up and help him remember how lucky and loved he really is.

In the park, a man is digging a hole to plant

a tree. He stands on the spade like it's a pogo stick, and jumps on it to push it further down into the grass. It is a big wide spade with a wooden handle and it glints in the light. It is the thing that gives me my best idea yet.

I am going to make Benny a present which is a wooden box full of gold coins and then I will bury it somewhere clever. We can make a trail and the invitations can be an actual true-to-life map. All of his friends can hide along the route, according to the map, like extra surprises, and then at the very end, when we are all together at Plane Tree Gardens, Benny can dig where X marks the spot, and find his buried present.

I know it's a great idea because I am fizzing with excitement about it. I can't wait to tell Grandad. Also, I need to ask him if I can dig a hole in North Korea so I can hide my box of coins there. I am thinking that if I put a nail or something metal inside it, Benny will be able to use his brand-new metal detector to locate it. I am very much hoping that Grandad's answer to the hole-digging question is going to be a yes. But when I get to 48 Plane Tree Gardens, he is not at home. I am so used to him dozing in his chair between four and five o'clock that I am not sure what to do. He has always been one hundred per cent reliable, apart from today. His newspaper is there, neatly folded, and his reading glasses, but no actual Grandad. He isn't cleaning something in the kitchen or ironing his underpants in his room, and he isn't out in the garden either, front or back.

He is absolutely nowhere.

Weirdly, it's Buster who is asleep on the

chair all alone in the middle of the afternoon, and Grandad who is nowhere in sight. They have switched places.

When I have given up on looking, I write a letter to my friend Fedor who wants to be a magician when he grows up. I tell him that a wizard might have put my grandad into the body of his own cat. I say that the cat is snoozing in an armchair, and I am on the lookout for an old man who can wash his own feet with his tongue and likes to sit under a honeysuckle bush and catch birds in his open mouth.

If Claude was home I would ask her to draw some pictures to go with my letter, but she is still at school because it is Thursday and she has Art Club. My sister is an extremely good artist. Her teacher is called Ms Feldner. She is from Bavaria and she is tall and angular like an ink drawing and wears mostly long black clothes so you can't see her feet. At parents' evening, Ms Feldner told Mum and Dad that even if Claude fell down the stairs and broke both her hands she would still get a 1 in art. When Dad can't remember her name he calls her Morticia.

Claude gets back just after five, in a bad mood. She sits in the kitchen, staring into space and eating biscuit after biscuit. When she asks me where the fascist dictators are, I say, 'I think they went to do a food shop.'

She rolls her eyes extravagantly. 'See? They even control what we *eat*.'

I ask her how her day has been, and she says, 'As rubbish as yesterday.'

'Was yesterday rubbish?' I ask, because I really don't think so, and she says, 'Yes, Joy. And before you ask, tomorrow will be as well.'

'Why will it?'

Claude's shoulders are as high up as her ears. 'It just will.' Then she sighs dramatically and says that Riddle is a mean rubbish person with an ego problem and she only stops sighing when she has another biscuit in her mouth.

'What did he do this time?' I ask her.

Claude starts counting Riddle's crimes on her fingers. 'He said I ate too much and he didn't like my trainers. He ignored me at first break. He will *not* stop looking at his own reflection. He is in love with the sound of his own voice and he thinks he's right and I'm wrong. All. The. Time.'

'Oh dear,' I say. 'He doesn't sound like much fun.'

'I have dumped him,' she says. 'He is history.'

'Well, *good*,' I tell her. 'That's very clever of you.' And I swear I see the tiniest glint in her eye which is the start of a smile.

I am just about to go out to the corner to post my letter to Fedor when I see Grandad strolling down the front path, w*histling*. This is not a thing I have ever heard him do before. When he comes into the kitchen, he takes off his hat and bows with a flourish like a prince in a cartoon.

'Hello, fair maidens,' he says, and Claude looks confused and says, 'Are you all right?'

'I am better than all right,' says Grandad. 'I am tickety-boo.'

'You're *what*?' Claude says.

'Tip top,' Grandad says. 'A-okay. I am the bee's knees.'

I think he has a leaf stuck in his hair. His cheeks are pink from the cold and I swear his eyes are *twinkling*.

'Have you been somewhere nice?' I say, hoping

that I know precisely where.

'Just out,' he says, winking at Claude, who shudders and grabs a handful of biscuits and starts going upstairs to our room.

I think it is a very good time to see if I can dig a hole in Grandad's garden to bury Benny's birthday present. All signs point to YES. And in fact when I ask him, he waves his arms around and says, 'Wonderful idea. I'm going to take up that concrete and dig the whole thing over and plant vegetables anyway.'

'What's got into him?' Claude says, coming back into the kitchen for her school bag just as Grandad goes out of the back door into the garden, twittering like a songbird.

I say nothing, because even though I'm hoping that he has been struck by a lightning bolt of love-at-first-sight for a certain green-fingered, cat-kidnapping neighbour, I don't actually know the full story. I think I'll sleep on it, and wait to find out if it might be true.

17

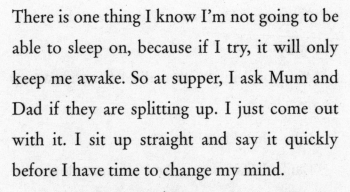

There is one thing I know I'm not going to be able to sleep on, because if I try, it will only keep me awake. So at supper, I ask Mum and Dad if they are splitting up. I just come out with it. I sit up straight and say it quickly before I have time to change my mind.

Mum blinks before she answers me. Dad has trouble swallowing his rice. Claude's face goes purple with the effort of not talking, and when

Buster disappears through the kitchen window, Grandad looks like he wants to disappear with him.

It is quiet for so long that I am starting to wish I hadn't asked.

Then Mum says, 'No, darling.'

'What gave you that idea?' Dad says, and I look at Claude, who says nothing. Her eyes are two ping-pong balls, but her mouth is a tight full-stop.

'I'm sorry,' Dad says. 'We are very busy and distracted.'

Mum joins in. 'With really boring grown-up stuff.'

'Like what?' I say.

'Banks,' Dad says. 'And job interviews and night shifts.'

'Medical records,' Mum says. 'And birth certificates and credit cards.'

'Not with divorce,' Dad says, and Mum nods. 'Not with *splitting up*.'

'Are you sure?' I say. 'Do you promise?'

They hold hands with me over the salt and pepper, and they speak at exactly the same time and they are smiling. 'Yes, we're sure, and, yes, we promise.'

Then Dad says, 'Not this week anyway,' and Mum laughs.

'GOOD,' I say, and Grandad starts breathing again and I ask Claude to pass me the mustard.

'Here,' she says, and her voice is a bit wobbly, and when I look at her, her eyes are filling with tears.

'What's the matter?' I say, and she shakes her head and her eyes fill up a bit more.

She takes a bite of a mushroom. She has

difficulty chewing it. I don't think it is easy to chew anything while you are trying your absolute hardest not to cry.

'Claude?' Mum says, and my sister looks at her.

'What's wrong, darling?' says Dad, and she looks at him too.

I am crossing everything that she is not going to start her answer with, 'Joy, please tell Mum and/or Dad . . .' and I am in luck, because she doesn't.

Instead she says, in a very small voice, 'I've been worried,' and saying it is like opening the door in the dam to let all the water flood through, and she is nothing but tears.

Mum and Dad get up at the same time to give her a hug. They wrap their arms around her at the dinner table, like half a giant octopus.

All I can see of Claude is her red hair.

On the other side of the window, Buster sits and licks his lips in the night air.

I look at Grandad. His top button is undone. His hair is bordering on what he would call scruffy.

And I can feel it in my bones, that everything on my list is about to change for the better.

This change happens pretty quickly, before even I am expecting it, because it turns out that my sister has been doing some digging of her own.

'Oh, by the way,' she says, when we are cleaning our teeth and getting into our pyjamas. 'I think you might be right about Benny and Clark Watson.'

'In what way?'

'I've been asking around at school.'

'You have?'

'First of all,' she says through her toothpaste, 'I spoke to Sam.'

Straight away this makes me nervous. 'Sam Hooper?' I say. 'Benny's Sam?'

'Yes, Benny's Sam.' Claude smiles at her own reflection in the mirror. She shows her teeth to herself and grins. 'He's nice,' she says, without moving her mouth. 'I like him. He said you are all planning a surprise party for Benny's birthday and he said I could help.'

I am not enjoying this conversation as much as Claude is. This is not a thing I can say very often. 'What else did he tell you?'

'He didn't know anything about any bullying. He was very surprised and he said he thought Benny was being all serious and secretive about your tree.'

My best friend's secret is out and I find myself

behaving quite like him, and staring at the floor. There is a hole in my sock and my little toe is poking out of it. For some strange reason, I think it looks frightened and alone. 'Benny didn't want to tell Sam,' I say. 'He didn't want him to know.'

Claude scowls and spits into the sink. 'Well, that's ridiculous. If someone was bullying you, I'd want to be the first to know about it.'

'You would?'

'Of course I would. You're my little sister. The only person who's allowed to be mean to you is *me*.'

'Thanks, Claude,' I say. I hug her really quickly, before she has time to stop me, and then I let go.

'You're welcome,' she says. 'Just don't make it weird.'

'I won't. I promise.'

'Anyway,' she carries on talking and teeth-

159

brushing, 'Sam won't be saying anything to Clark Watson.'

'Why not?'

She smiles at herself again. 'Because *I* told him what Jojo told *me*.'

I don't know who Jojo is, but I am in too much of a hurry to ask anything else except, 'Which was what?'

Claude says that according to this person called Jojo, Jet and Clark's mum is not very well. 'Like *a lot* not very well,' she says. She looks serious and I know she means it.

'Oh.'

'Like off the charts, Joy.'

'Oh *no*.'

She says that Jojo says that Jet Watson has had to get a job after school to help with money problems. 'And Clark has to do everything at home, all the cooking and cleaning and shopping and the trying to look after their mum.'

I don't know what to say yet so I keep quiet.

'It's a LOT,' Claude says. And I know she is right. I am sure that this is much closer to the full story, which is that Clark Watson is sad and tired and lonely and worried and jealous of people like me and Benny who can walk home and up the stairs at Sunningdale without carrying four heavy bags and can sit on the swings eating crisps or go to the fair or try to feed parakeets or watch cartoons or dig for treasure, because we have all the spare time in the world. I am convinced that this is the main reason why he has stopped being friends with Benny and started throwing stuff and being mean to him everywhere instead.

Clark Watson needs some help. And even I can see that it is more help than Benny and I can give him.

The banner from Year Five's assembly is still burning my eyes and reminding me that the best way to deal with difficult things is to go ahead and *say* them.

SPEAK UP, BE KIND AND TELL THE TRUTH! HELP SOMEBODY TODAY.

The very least we can do, tomorrow at school, first thing, is *start*.

18

As soon as I see Benny, I tell him the new information about Clark that I found out from Claude. I don't tell him that she has spoken to Sam. I do say that what's going on in Clark's family must be the reason he is being so mean and angry. Benny doesn't shrug and read the blurb on my juice box, but he also doesn't say much. I'm sure it must be hard for him to understand his own bully, or feel even a little bit

163

sorry for him, but I am hoping this will happen sooner or later. I am leaving these new facts to filter down through the rock of Benny's brain, the way rainwater gets filtered by rocks until it is sweet and clean enough to drink.

While it is filtering, I warn him that something strange is probably going to happen in the very near future, but please can he trust me when I say everything will be okay.

'What are you talking about?' he says.

'I'm talking about the Clark Watson problem,' I tell him, and he looks at me out of the side of his eyes and just about mumbles. 'Oh. Okay.'

I say that I am determined to be nice to Clark, given the circumstances, the first chance I get, and that even though it might not seem that way to Benny, he is still my absolute all-time favourite best friend ever, and I am one hundred per cent doing it for *him*.

Benny nods quickly, but he doesn't meet my eye.

And when Clark comes up right behind us on the way back to 6C, I take the leap and say, 'Hello, Clark.'

Even with my special warning, Benny is not prepared for that. He stops dead in his tracks. He shudders to a halt like a sleeper train. His eyes are big and round and the scar on his forehead has completely vanished.

'What are you doing?' he hisses at me out of one side of his mouth.

'Are you talking to me?' Clark asks in his quiet playground voice.

'Yes,' I say, and I smile as hard as I can. My face feels like it is frozen. Clark Watson makes his way round Benny like he is a bollard. I notice that he does not smile back.

Benny still hasn't moved. He looks at me like I have betrayed him. He says in a fierce whisper, '*What is going on?*'

'*Trust me*,' I whisper back, and when he follows me into the classroom, I cross my fingers and I really hope I have got this right.

It actually isn't long before my next chance happens. In fact, it is miraculously quick. This term, we have been learning about the Victorians. Mrs Hunter is reading to us about the life of a scullery maid. This is a girl not much older than Claude who sleeps under the kitchen table and scrubs floors and cleans fires and does laundry in a big sink and heats water for other people to have their baths. I am keeping it zipped about how that still happens in lots of places, even now, and isn't just a thing from two hundred years ago, and I am doing this because I know it's what Mrs Hunter wants from me.

She says, 'Most Victorians didn't have showers and all the modern conveniences you all take for granted. They used a jug and basin to keep themselves clean. And went to the public baths. And would have maybe had a tin bath at home less than once a week.'

'*Ewwwwww*,' says half of 6C. And then Bailey Parker, who is a big boy with freckles like grains of sand, says loud enough for everyone to hear, 'That's more baths than Clark Watson has,' and he holds his nose and wafts the air like he is waving a bad smell away.

One half of 6C giggles. The other half looks shocked, and a bit glad Bailey Parker isn't talking about them. Mrs Hunter's lips go tight like they are stuck together with glue. This usually happens before she says something very cross and sends someone to the headteacher.

Clark Watson is wide eyed and as red as a berry. This is the first time I have noticed that his jumper is grubby and his trousers have a hole in them and his shoes look as muddy as if he came to school through a swamp. He stares at the ground like he is wishing the swamp would appear right now and swallow him whole.

I don't have a moment to waste. I look Mrs Hunter straight in the eye and I say, without putting my hand up, at the top of my voice. 'Oh, that's NOTHING. When we went trekking in the Himalayas I didn't see a bath for ONE WHOLE MONTH.'

I look over at Benny and open my eyes really

wide. I am silently willing him to join in, but he doesn't. He looks scared and lost and a bit angry. Now, both halves of 6C are pointing at me and laughing, which is fine with me, because it means they have already forgotten about how many times Clark Watson might or might not be washing in a week, and that was my plan.

Mrs Hunter nods at me. It is very quick and almost unnoticeable. For the first time in my school life so far, she does not tell me off for calling out and interrupting in class. She makes everyone close their mouths and sit on their hands, and for the rest of the time she is reading, we are quieter than mice.

When the bell goes, Mrs Hunter asks Bailey Parker to stay behind, and the rest of us file out one by one and in silence like a snake in the long grass. In the lunch queue, Benny and I are perilously close to Clark Watson, and I can feel Benny being very uncomfortable about it. He grips onto his packed lunch extra tight. It is egg and cress, his favourite, and I am guessing he doesn't want to lose it.

'What was that all about in class?' he asks me.

'Bailey Parker shouldn't have done that,' I say. 'It was unkind. It was mean.'

'Yeah, but Clark's mean too,' Benny says. 'Why did you stick up for him?'

'I told you,' I said. 'I'm going to be Clark Watson's friend however I can, however mean he is being.'

'*Ssshhh*,' Benny says, because he doesn't want Clark to notice we are talking about him. He doesn't want us to be noticed at all.

I whisper back, '*Sorry*.'

'What do you think being out-of-the-blue nice

to him is going to do?' Benny says. 'Make him instantly stop bullying me?'

'Of course not,' I tell him, and Benny clamps his jaw shut and nods his head, like what I'm doing is useless, and he is right and he has made his point.

'It can't hurt, though,' I say.

'What do you mean?'

'Well, being kind to him might not make things better straight away, but it definitely won't make things worse.'

Benny mumbles. 'They can't get much worse.'

'Exactly. So next time it's your turn.'

My best friend looks at me like I have been replaced by a replica and he is only just realizing it.

'*My* turn?' he says. 'My? *Turn?*'

'Yes. If you feel like it, I mean.'

Just then, one of the boys from 6F comes past

171

us with Bailey Parker and when they see Clark Watson they hold their noses and the boy from 6F whose name is Steven Richards says something about raw sewage and Bailey laughs and Clark turns red as a berry again and frowns at the floor.

I look at Benny and Benny looks at me.

The banner is right above our heads. It runs the length of the room from the door to the lunch counter. **SPEAK UP. BE KIND AND TELL THE TRUTH! HELP SOMEBODY TODAY!**

Benny swallows. He clenches his fists. I swear his feet push into the floor and he gets a tiny bit taller.

'BAILEY,' he calls after them, and Bailey and Steven Richards turn and smile. They both like Benny, because he is so good at running and football, and because he is just so completely easy to like.

Clark Watson stops frowning at his shoes. He

is watching. I know this because I am watching him back. Quite a few people are. The queue is quieter than normal. Bailey and Steven Richards are starting to look uncomfortable.

Benny takes a deep breath. 'Not kind,' he says.

Bailey acts confused. 'Huh? What?'

Benny shrugs. 'You heard me.' He is pointing up at the banner. 'Leave him alone.'

Now it is Bailey's turn to glare at his own footwear. He looks ashamed. Steven Richards puts his hands in his pockets and sort of edges away from him. And before Bailey can say anything back to Benny, the queue moves and it is our turn to go and sit down at a table and so we are gone.

I haven't taken my eyes off Clark Watson. He looks like he has just woken up somewhere and isn't sure where that somewhere is. He doesn't speak to us, but he is staring at Benny sort of like he hasn't really seen him before. Benny nods at Clark, the way Mrs Hunter nodded at me, and Clark nods back. It isn't a sorry or a thank-you, but it does feel like something. It definitely feels like a start.

Benny unwraps his sandwich and I tell him he's brave. He takes a big bite and I tell him he's generous. His glasses slide down his nose and almost into his egg and cress and he looks at me and laughs. Just like the old Benny.

A shadow looms over us. I'm not sure how long it's been looming before we see it.

'Joy Applebloom,' the shadow says. It is Mrs Hunter.

The old Benny stops laughing.

Mrs Hunter's hair is tied up in a bun and strands of it are coming loose. Her glasses have made a red welt on the bridge of her nose and she is pinching it. She looks like she could do with a hot water bottle and an afternoon on the sofa, just like Claude does when she is sick. She is a long way up, like a giraffe, or a giant redwood tree, from where we are sitting.

She says, 'I want to talk to you about what just happened in our classroom.'

'I'm sorry I called out,' I tell her. 'I know you don't like it but I wanted to—'

Mrs Hunter closes her eyes and breathes through her nose like she often does when I am talking. It makes her look like a patient and very worn-out horse. It makes me stop.

'Sorry,' I tell her, just to make sure she heard me the first time.

'I haven't come to tell you off,' she says.

'Really?'

'I have come to say thank you.'

Mrs Hunter smiles. It is a bit alarming. I look at Benny and his eyebrows are hovering like flying saucers above the frames of his glasses.

'*Thank you?*' we say at the exact same time.

'Yes, Joy. I know why you spoke up in the classroom like that, and it is just the sort of behaviour we are striving for in this school. You are a very kind and very outspoken girl.'

And then she walks away, leaving me so surprised, I almost forget how to eat my own lunch.

'Did that just happen?' Benny says.

'I think so.'

'She's right,' Benny says. 'You are very kind.'

'I am?'

'Yes. And speaking up for Clark Watson felt good. It was the right thing. And it's either that or the sandwich, but I'm starting to feel better already.'

19

Next time we go to Sunningdale, I ask Benny's mum if she knows the Watsons. I do it while Benny is chopping pineapple and I am making coconut icing. He doesn't know it, but we are doing a trial run for his birthday cake. Angela is whisking egg-whites in a big shiny bowl. I speak quietly so Benny won't hear me over the clatter of her beads.

'From downstairs?' I say. 'From number 9?'

Angela frowns. Her voice is hushed too. 'Yes,' she says. 'I do. Lovely family. It's very sad.'

'Is she very ill?' I say. 'Their mum?'

Angela looks at me. 'Who told you that?'

'Claude,' I said. 'She's at school with Jet.'

'She doesn't want people to know at the moment,' Angela says. 'So I haven't told anyone. I've been going over there now and then when the boys are at school. You know, keeping her company, doing the odd thing around the house. Oh! That reminds me, I said I'd go to the launderette for her tomorrow. Those boys are wearing out their clothes.'

'Do you know Clark?' I say.

'Of course. We've known Clark since he was born, haven't we, Benny?'

Benny doesn't look up. He isn't listening and he can't hear us. Clark hasn't thrown anything at

178

Benny for nearly a whole week now. He hasn't pushed him over or 'borrowed' his money. He even managed to 'find' Benny's phone down the back of a bookshelf in 6C, and when he gave it back there wasn't a scratch on it. And this afternoon, in the playground, when Benny and I were sitting under our thousand-year-old tree, Clark came up to us and sat down too.

Benny's shoulders went stiff and he sat sort of bolt upright like he was waiting for something horrible to happen.

'It's okay,' Clark said, in his quiet voice, and we both leaned in a bit closer to hear him. 'I'm not here to cause trouble, I promise.'

'What are you here for, then?' Benny said. He pushed his glasses back up and frowned the way he does when he's trying to see something really close up.

 179

Clark coughed a bit, like he was getting ready. He wiped the palms of his hands on his coat. He seemed nervous.

'Are you all right, Clark?' I said.

He nodded. 'Yes, I think so,' and then he looked straight at Benny. 'I've come to apologize,' he said.

Benny opened his mouth but he didn't say anything. No words came out. He looked like Benny, if Benny was born a fish.

Clark Watson said, 'I understand if you never want to be my friend again but I just wanted you to know that I'm very, *very* sorry.'

Fish Benny nodded, and when he and Clark shook hands on it, I smiled until I thought my face was going to fall off. And then, as quick as he'd sat down, he got up and left us under the tree.

'That was nice of him,' I said.

'Wow,' Benny said back, and after that he didn't talk for a bit. 'Just *wow.*'

At the Hoopers' house, in their kitchen, while Angela beats egg whites and Benny eats as much pineapple as he chops, I take my chance, speaking quickly and quietly. I know I haven't asked his permission. I can't do that without ruining the big surprise. So I am taking matters into my own hands. It's a risk but I think it is the right thing to do.

'Could we invite Clark to Benny's party?' I say. 'Do you think he'd like to come?'

Angela puts the bowl down on the counter and wipes her hands on a tea towel.

'Great idea,' she says, and she winks at me. 'He'll love that. I'll add him to the list.'

At home I have been even more busy with

my to-do pile of letters than normal. As well as all my other ones, I have had more than thirty party invitations to write for Benny's birthday. Claude helped me with the design. Each envelope opens like a treasure chest, and the card inside is the treasure. There is a map of the trail that Angela and Ed have planned out, with gold coins marking ten spots. It is one of my jobs to tell people which spots to be on, and at what time. Everyone is going to leap out and surprise him as he goes along. And at the end, which is 48 Plane Tree Gardens, Benny is going to dig up his treasure.

This part is extremely, eye-wateringly exciting and very hard to keep quiet about. Because Grandad has done something incredible. He has bought a real life actual Roman coin on the internet and it has arrived and it is buried in the garden in my wooden box with some other chocolate coins, a horseshoe that we dug up when we were making new flower beds, and an egg cup that Claude drew a picture of Benny on, which is really quite realistic.

A real Roman coin.

I write a letter to my friend Maria in Madrid, telling her all about it. I say, *It has been a very busy time. I have been juggling a few things but I haven't dropped any. And this is going to be the best surprise birthday treasure hunt ever.*

All of 6C is invited. And my whole family. Grandad asked if he could bring a *friend*, and his eyes twinkled when he said it. I am excited for Mum and Dad to get to know Angela and Ed a bit better. And Claude won't admit it, but I know she is looking forward to seeing Sam.

And Clark Watson is definitely coming. I know he is, because I delivered his invitation by hand, and he said about forty-three thank-yous and he promised his answer was yes.

Dear ...

You are
TOP SECRETLY
invited to
BENNY'S BIRTHDAY
SURPRISE TREASURE HUNT
on Sunday 1st August.
Your number on the trail is ...
Please be there at ....
And REMEMBER,
don't say a word!

Love from Joy x

Acknowledgements

THANK YOU to Veronique Baxter, Rachel Denwood, Lowri Ribbons, David McDougall and Claire Lefevre. And thank you to Luky Chanian for the stick and the glass.

Letter-writing Tips from JOY

1. Make sure the paper you choose matches the person you are writing to. For instance, my letter to Miss Wolfe was very garden-y and green, with flowers and bugs down the side. But I wouldn't send that to Claude.

2. If you don't have fancy stationery, it is actually more fun to decorate your own. I like to doodle on my letters, along the top and bottom, down the sides, and sometimes even in the middle of a sentence.

3. (This one includes the envelopes, too.) I love sending letters that also look like works of art. I draw crowns and balloons on people's names, and if I'm sending a birthday card, there are always candles and cake. Envelopes are fine as long as the address is right and you can still read it. I like to think my drawings make the post-people smile.

4. Sometimes I send sweets and stickers and sometimes I send seashells and other stuff I've found. Lots of my friends own a leaf or an acorn from my favourite old oak tree. Letters with little presents in them are even more fun to receive.

5. Start with your name and address in the top right hand corner. Just in case the person

you are writing to has forgotten it and really wants to write back. Stack it up in a sort of square like a pile of bricks.

6. Remember to put the date underneath too. Imagine, in hundreds of years, your letters might end up in a museum as actual relics of an ancient time.

7. If you are writing to a friend, you can say, 'Hello! It's me!' But if you are writing to someone else less friendly (AKA Mrs Hunter), start your letter with 'Dear . . .' as in 'Dear Mrs Hunter'. Not 'Hi, Mrs Hunter. How's it going?'

8. Tell your news and remember to ask questions. It improves your chances of getting a reply.

9. It is important that you get exactly the right stamp. They come in all shapes and sizes and cost different amounts of money. Sometimes they are a bit plain and simple, and sometimes they have lovely pictures on them. Sometimes

you need quite a few. It costs a lot more to send something far away and heavy than it does to send something quite light in the same country as you, and if you want your letter to get there safely, you have to get that bit right. I like weighing my letters at the post office. They have a shiny scale and they also have pretend letterboxes to make sure what you send isn't too bulging with surprises to fit through.

10. There are lots of different ways to end a letter. If I was writing to Joseph or Prosper in Tanzania, I might say *Tutaonana Baadaye*, because that means 'see you later' in Swahili. If I was writing to Anita in Delhi, I could say *dher saara pyar*, because that's 'LOTS of love,' in Hindi. My friend Fedor always signs his letters *Doei, bestie. Tot ziens*, which means 'Bye, bestie. See you later'. For more serious and grown-up things you are supposed to say, 'Yours sincerely' or 'Yours faithfully' or 'Best regards'. But most of the time I just write 'Love from Joy'.

Look out
for more
JOY

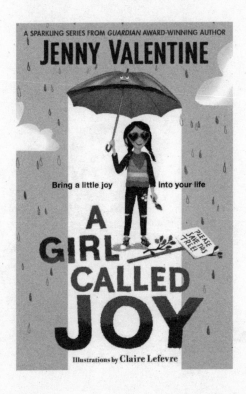

A SPARKLING SERIES FROM *GUARDIAN* AWARD-WINNING AUTHOR

JENNY VALENTINE

Bring a little joy   into your life

A
GIRL
CALLED
JOY

PLEASE SAVE THIS TREE!

Illustrations by Claire Lefevre

Turn the page for a sneak peek
from Joy's first adventure!

1

There is absolutely no storybook magic in our family. We don't have a grandad who can fly, or an uncle who is busy somewhere building a time machine, or parents who are world-famous wizards-in-hiding. Our grandad walks with a stick, we have zero uncles, and our mum and dad have out-of-the-blue started saying things like, 'Put that back where it came from,' and, 'Where's your school uniform?' and,

'Please hoover your room immediately.'

According to my big sister, Claude, this makes us extremely ordinary. But we have never been ordinary. And I don't think we should be ready to start now.

I'm not pretending there haven't been some big changes. Things are feeling very pedestrian around here, that's for sure. Extremely squidged in. And it goes without saying that nobody has a wand to get us out of trouble, or their own super-helpful pack of wolves, or a lump of rock that can speak in whole sentences. There are no parallel universes under our sinks, or other worlds in our wardrobes, or perfect tiny humans between our walls. There are cleaning products, and clothes, and possibly mice. I don't have shoes that rush about all over the place with a mind of their own. I have one pair of trainers that are at least one size too small, and I am not ready to throw them away yet because they have been with me everywhere, on so many adventures. The washing machine won't get the grass stains out of Claude's precious new jeans, and right now, Dad can't get rid of the coffee he spilled on Grandad's carpet. So I am pretty sure that none of us can make stuff disappear.

But the thing is, there is more than one kind of magic. It shouldn't have to mean the same as *impossible*, and only be allowed to happen in stories. That just doesn't seem right to me. Claude says our definitions of magic are different, and that I am always marvelling at something or other for no good reason because I am way too easily impressed. I am twenty-four seven on the lookout for some everyday, actually real-life magic because that's the kind I believe in, and, to be honest, I think we could do with some.

When I say so, Claude does one of her semi-professional eye-rolls and says, 'Oh, yeah? Well. Good luck with that.'

When you don't have storybook magic, your problems are less fancy and not as much fun to fix. For example, Dad has stuck a big heavy book about trees over the coffee stain, in a hurry, and now it is lurking there in the middle of the room where it doesn't belong, like a suitcase in a canal. Any minute, somebody, most likely Grandad, is going to bump into it and find out the truth. Claude says it's not going to be pretty when he does, and it is only a matter of time. Even with my talent for positive thinking, I am starting to think she might have got that one right.

I am ten, and Claude is thirteen.

She smells like cherries and wears black make-up all over her eyes. She has the straightest, whitest teeth and the shiniest toothpaste smile I have ever seen. When she is happy, she looks like an advert for the dentist, but at the moment that isn't very often. Dad says Claude's toothpaste smile has become a bit like a meteor shower, because it might only happen once or twice a year, and if you blink you'll miss it.

We saw a meteor shower in California, when I was six and Claude was nine. The sky rained stars for hours and hours, and I fell asleep before it was finished. You would have to do a long old blink to miss that.

Claude is short for Claudia Eloise, and

rhymes with bored, which these days is just about right. Ever since we got back to the UK and moved into Grandad's house, she is always complaining that nothing is worth doing and there is less than nothing to do. Mum and Dad have started calling her *the brick wall*, but not so she can hear them. They whisper it behind their hands, but I'm not sure they need to bother. As far as I can tell, she has pretty much completely stopped listening to anything they have to say.

Mum and Dad's names are Rina and Dan, short for Marina Jane Blake and Daniel Samson Applebloom. They have been hyper-distracted and crazy-busy since we arrived, doing out-of-character and mind-bendingly ordinary things like applying for jobs that involve zero travel, signing up at the doctor's, and shoe-horning us into schools. These are not activities we are used to our parents being busy at. In fact, they are the total opposite of what we have spent our whole lives being taught to expect. It is very unsettling. Claude reckons Mum and Dad had radical personality transplants, like, overnight, when we weren't looking. She says they might not actually be our original parents any more, and we need to stay alert, because absolutely anything could be about to happen.

I say, 'Are you sure they're the only ones?' because right now I would bet money on the fact she's had the personality transplant too. She definitely isn't acting like my original sister. She isn't nearly as much fun as she used to be.

I haven't had anything transplanted. I am exactly the same as ever, even though everything else has changed. My name can't be shortened and I don't have a middle one. It is what it is, and everyone just calls me Joy.

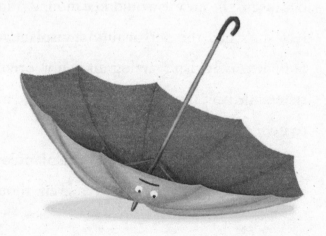

2

The here that we have got to is Grandad's house.

His name is Thomas Blake, and he is Mum's dad, although sometimes I find it hard to believe they are even related. I would never ever pick them out of a line-up of fathers and daughters, unless I knew. Not in a million. Grandad is sort of faint and blurry, like someone drew him with a soft pencil, and Mum is marker-pen dark. Mum is loud and bombastic and colourful, and Grandad is more narrow and faded and quiet. Mum is a socialist, which is a long political word for being good-at-sharing, and Grandad? Well, Grandad is not. Mum says we are world citizens and should support the free movement of people across the globe, and I think Grandad would prefer to put a nice tall fence around this one little island, and cover it in great big signs that say,

NO TRESPASSING

and

PRIVATE PROPERTY

and

KEEP OUT.

Our family does not see eye to eye with Grandad on a long list of things. I think that's why we spend so much time talking to him about the weather.

The letters on his doormat say Mr T. E. Blake but he won't tell me what the E is for, so I have decided to guess. I have been allowing myself a new guess every day. I don't think I am close to getting it right, but so far he has not decided to correct me, so I'm just going to carry on trying.

Thomas Elephant Blake's face is full of pockets and pouches like a backpack and when he speaks, the pockets and pouches fill and empty with air. The letters he gets are mostly catalogues for slippers that plug into the wall, and baths with actual doors in the side for getting in and out, and hearing aids disguised as reading glasses. I think the catalogues are brilliant and inventive, but Thomas Eggcup Blake does not agree. He says that having permanently cold feet and not being able to climb in and out of the bath or hear and see properly are not reasons to celebrate. I think he says that about a lot of things. I'm not sure he is really the celebrating kind. He is mostly grey from head to toe, like he has just walked through a room where the ceiling fell in. Claude says that wouldn't happen at Thomas Eagle-Eye Blake's house, where everything looks scared of being out of place. She says the ceilings wouldn't be brave enough. They actually wouldn't dare.

Mum is keen for us all to get along like a house on fire, another thing my sister says would never happen, seeing as Grandad goes around at night switching every single plug socket off. We aren't supposed to make up our minds about him yet, because we don't know him well enough to reach a proper verdict. Mum says, Family is Family is Family, whatever side of the fence you're on, whatever your domestic habits or whatever you believe. Dad says we all need to be patient with each other, and spend more time together, and let the dust settle.

Claude says, 'Fat chance,' and I think, 'What dust? There isn't even one speck,' but they both say that it will be worth the wait, and that eventually the real Grandad will emerge like a butterfly coming out of its chrysalis, or at least a snake shedding its old skin.

I have seen thousands and thousands of Monarch butterflies hatching in Mexico, turning the hillsides a living, quivering red, and I have watched a rattlesnake leave behind its own skin outside in the hot sand, quick and papery as a crayon wrapper. So I wonder exactly how soon and how spectacular Thomas Extravaganza Blake's big reveal might actually be.

Claude shakes her head at me, and then at Mum and Dad, and then at our new squashed-in world in general, and says something muffled and full of gravel about nobody bothering to hold their breath.

3

Before we landed here, we had always travelled about. A lot. The four of us have been moving and living and working and mucking about in all sorts of parts of the world since I was a baby, since before I can even remember. Claude and Mum and Dad and me. We have always been free as birds. Claude keeps a list somewhere, in one of her many notebooks, of all the different places we have been, and I've forgotten the exact number, but there are 195 countries in the world and counting, so we were only just getting started.

Grandad likes to call what we did 'gallivanting about the globe'. Mum and Dad always called it 'living'.

Before, if we were a family of plants, we would have been sycamore blades or maple keys or those bits of dandelion fluff that float along on the breeze from one place to another, minding their own business, going places, never worrying where.

Mum used to watch the sunset over wherever we were, and sigh in a good way and say, 'Aren't we lucky?' She used to say she could never see us stuck in one place, in a box, on a street with identical boxes, all nailed down.

And the rest of us agreed.

When it was hard to leave stuff behind, there were always new things ahead of us to make up for it. The giggling sisters in the café in Hanoi that makes the sweet soup, or the elephant boats in Mumbai, or Fabiola, the girl in Mexico City who taught me Spanish at the exact same time as teaching me how to roller-skate, so that I didn't even realize until later that I was learning to do both.

And if problems started to mount up, such as giant mosquito bites, or genuine real-life cooked guinea pigs on the menu, or traffic fumes as thick and damp as cotton wool, then moving day was a very handy thing that could not come fast enough.

So far, I have grown up always looking forward to what's next. For as long as I can remember, there has been something interesting to do and somewhere exciting to be right around the corner.

The four of us have liked it that way, and I've never known anything else, which is why Mum and Dad say it's no surprise that I'm the sunniest, most adventurous person they know.

Look out
for more
JOY

coming soon!